Rise of Dragons – Book 5

Attack on Avalon

G Clatworthy

Find more at *www.gemmaclatworthy.com*

Cover art by Sanjay Charlon (Beehive Illustrations)

Foreword

This story takes place in the Rise of Dragons universe; a world where magical and mundane beings coexist and dragons have recently been awoken.

The first three books in the Rise of Dragons series are told from the point of view of Amethyst Haernson, a half-dwarf jeweller who just wants a quiet life. Book 4 shows Special Agent Ruth Jones' point of view and is set in parallel to the end of Book 2 and part of Book 3. In this book, we're back to Amethyst's point of view. Now we're all caught up, read on…

If you want to support Gemma, you can find her on patreon.com/G_Clatworthy for exclusive first reads of new stories. You can also join her newsletter for a free prequel to this series and follow Gemma on www.instagram.com/gemmaclatworthy, www.facebook.com/gemmaclatworthy or join the reader's group Gemma's book wyrms.

Chapter 1

"Slow the dzrak down!" I used the Dwarfish curse word with ease.

"We're fine," my gnomish friend was blasé about her speed as she hurled the van around a corner so fast I swear two of the wheels left the ground.

"You're going to get us killed!"

"You want to get there on time don't you?"

I grabbed the 'oh schiztz' handle above the window tightly. I wasn't so sure I wanted to get there at all. We were hurtling towards the elven tree city of Breconia. The last time I had been there, a chimera had tried to kill me and a dragon had gate crashed the annual Equinox Ball. Still, I was beginning to think I'd rather take my chances with the dragon. I watched the scenery pass with a blur as Aloora overtook a tractor at breakneck speed. She reached a hand over and squeezed my knee. She knew I was nervous.

"Get your hands back on the wheel!"

With a smile and a shrug, she put both hands back onto the steering wheel and accelerated harder. I closed my eyes and tried to ignore the sinking feeling in my stomach. We were on our way to attend the memorial service for the late King Lireath. I had been standing next to him when he had been killed by the ice dragon in a fit of fury.

"I don't know why you're going if you're feeling so bad. I wouldn't waste any time on that, that, dzrakbar!"

I blinked at my friend. That was a serious Dwarfish curse word that juxtaposed oddly with her pixie haircut and wide blue eyes.

"I'm not going for me, I'm going for Lorandir." Despite my foreboding, my lips turned up slightly at the mention of the handsome elf. My boyfriend. I still couldn't quite believe we were together and if he needed my support for his uncle's memorial, I would be there.

"You romantic," she turned to give me a smile. The van veered onto the other side of the road.

"Keep your eyes on the road!"

With a shake of her head, Aloora steered us back to our own side of the main road winding towards the elven city. She shook her fist at a lorry driver who had beeped us and carried on. Then she swore softly under her breath in one of the many languages she spoke. I raised my eyebrow and redoubled my grip on the plastic handle as she pulled sharply into a layby. The van's wheels screeched across the gravel and we came to an abrupt stop. The blue lights of a police car flashed behind us. I groaned and tried to look inconspicuous. Aloora smoothed her tartan dress and sat up straight with a perky smile playing across her lips.

The officer rapped on the window with his knuckle and signalled for Aloora to wind it down.

"Driving licence please."

"Of course Officer Gorgeous," she held out the small pink card that was her licence along with the paper counterpart. I could have sworn she winked too. I looked straight ahead to stop my mouth dropping open.

"It's Officer Greguz, are you insured to drive this vehicle?"

"Absolutely," she pulled out some more paperwork and handed it over smoothly with a smile. I wondered how many times she had been stopped by the police in her brief time driving. The Officer gave it a cursory glance and made a note on the pad of paper he was carrying.

"Were you aware of the speed at which you were driving?"

"Yes."

"So you know you were going at seventy miles an hour?"

"Oh yes."

"In a fifty mile an hour zone. That's an automatic suspension of your driving licence," he glanced at the pink card in his hand, "which you've held for just a year I see."

Aloora gave up all pretence at flirting, "Hmmm, not if I'm on official business for the Magical Liaison Office, which I am. On an urgent assignment, which I am. We're heading to Breconia, which, as you may know, is now home to a number of dragons, which fall under our jurisdiction or more specifically mine as the assigned Agent," she flashed her I.D at the officer.

His eyes widened. This was clearly not something he dealt with every day. He made a show of reading the I.D. "Can someone confirm your assignment?"

Aloora nodded and handed him Agent Jones' business card with a flourish.

"Ruth Jones huh?"

I almost felt sorry for the young police officer calling up the head of the Welsh branch of the Magical Liaison Office. She was not known for her patience.

He dialled the number, "What's occurring?"

He winced and held the phone away from his face as the shifter lambasted him for his poor Gavin and Stacey joke. He actually turned red and twisted his foot on the ground like a disgruntled toddler.

"I see..." he handed Aloora back the I.D and the other documents. My friend tucked them away neatly back into the pocket on the driver's door. The officer looked over at me. I smiled nervously. What is it about police officers that make you feel nervous even if you've done nothing wrong? His eyes dropped to the foot well and narrowed. I looked down. Schiztz. My double-headed axe was lying under my feet, glinting slightly in the early morning sunshine.

"You got a permit for that?"

"Er..."

Aloora came to my rescue, "It's a cultural weapon. My friend is a dwarf, which as you know gives her the right to carry a mining tool or other tool of cultural significance."

"That's an axe!"

"Yes, exactly. A tool for chopping wood, very handy down the mines I'm sure."

"It's got two sides!"

"Yes, you can chop twice as much wood before needing to sharpen it. Those dwarves are an ingenious people are they not?"

The officer shook his head, "I suppose she's on this official business with you?"

Aloora smiled brightly and held out another card. He frowned and then waved it away, "Alright, I'm letting you go. Drive safely and I will be following up with your superior." He stomped back to his car. Aloora had the presence of mind to let the police car drive off first before pulling back out onto the road.

We had gone about five miles at a slightly more sedate pace, which meant we weren't careening around corners on two wheels, when Aloora's phone rang. She dug it out of a pocket and tossed it to me. I fumbled the catch and it dropped by my feet, still blurting out the Ride of the Valkyries ring tone. I retrieved the large phone and answered it just in time. Agent Jones' voice blared from the device.

"Why am I getting calls from the police this early in the morning Dragonquest?!"

I winced at her sharp voice, "Er, actually it's me, Amethyst. Aloora's driving. I'll put you on speaker."

"Do you want to tell me why the police just called?"

"Nothing to worry about, we just had a slight disagreement about driving speeds. It's all sorted." Aloora's voice was breezy as she overtook a tractor.

"And why pray tell were you driving so fast?"

"We've got to get to the memorial service in time. I don't want to let the Office down."

"The service isn't until one p.m.! That's three hours away!"

"I don't want to be late..."

"Stop talking. I can see from the GPS tracker that you'll get there with plenty of time to spare. Slow down and stick to the speed limit! Don't make me take you off the van's registered driver list!" Agent Jones hung up.

My friend swore softly, "Dzrak it, I forgot about the inbuilt GPS. Do you think she'd really stop me driving Dan?" She gave the dashboard a little pat as she said the van's name.

"No idea, but maybe you should slow down!"

With a sigh, Aloora eased off the accelerator and slowed to something approaching the speed limit. She began drumming the steering wheel in time with the song on the radio as if she was bored. I shook my head at her newly found speed demon tendencies and went back to staring out of the window.

As we approached the Breconian reserve that housed the city, a familiar mist surrounded the van. The elves had been thorough. It was designed to keep the multitude of magical creatures that called the reserve home in, and anyone with negative intentions towards the elves out. Aloora slowed the vehicle to a crawl as visibility reduced to a few feet in front of the windscreen.

I leaned forward and peered out of the window, unable to stop the uneasy feeling creeping up my spine. I couldn't help but remember the tarfangtula attack earlier in the year. I shivered at the thought of the hideous ten-legged creatures swarming the van. Was that a shadow in the mist?

I blinked and the swirling fog changed shape again.

Chapter 2

As abruptly as it had appeared, the mist cleared, revealing no monstrous creatures. I shook my head at my own overactive imagination. We were in the reserve. We hadn't been attacked. It was all good.

Aloora manoeuvred the van into a parking space on the sand-coloured car park. Vehicles weren't allowed further into the reserve and the car park was already half full. I guessed the vehicles I could see were for guests who had stayed overnight. I let myself out of the van and hefted my backpack over one shoulder and my axe over the other. I tried not to stare at the deep purple Rolls Royce with pink highlights. No one said elves had to have taste.

We walked towards an elf in a grey uniform with gold trim. An opal-coloured portal shimmered behind him with small gryphgeons milling around it. Some of the small catlike creatures were pawing the ground, a few were sitting down, looking regal as they preened their golden fur and feathers, and one was pecking at the ground with its pigeon sized beak. I guess you could say they were the equivalent of carrier pigeons, if carrier pigeons could maul you with their claws.

One of the smaller convertibles seemed to hum with magical modifications. I eyed it nervously as we squeezed past it but it did nothing more than vibrate slightly. The cars almost made me forget that we were at the top of a cliff with a sharp drop down into a green valley that lay between the car park and the forest where the elven city lay.

The tall elf eyed us with a sneer as we approached, taking in our appearance. Aloora was in a black skater style dress with dark fishnet tights and chunky black boots with small dragons embroidered on them. His eyes lingered on the golden collar at her neck. I was proud of that piece of jewellery: I had hammered the gold to give it a more weathered, ancient feel and set a single dragon scale into it. It was the first item forged with any dragon power in millennia and my friend insisted on wearing it all the time.

I was wearing one of my corset style tops with a cardigan under my favourite red leather jacket, with a long, tiered black skirt as a nod to the mourning in the memorial service. His eyes stopped as they took in my gothic style leather boots with their thick soles and several scratches. I shifted my skirt so it hid the comfortable, but in no way smart, footwear. His eyes flicked back to our faces, “Name.”

Aloora drew herself up to her full height, about an inch taller than me. She came up to the elf’s chest. “Aloora Dragonquest, representative of the Magical Liaison Office and Amethyst Haernson, girlfriend to Prince Lorandir.”

“Er, I don’t know that he’s a prince exactly…” I interrupted my friend and played with my own necklace nervously. The large dark purple stone - an amethyst, my namesake stone - calmed me a little. She ignored me.

The elf's eyes narrowed slightly as he gave me another appraising look, no doubt surprised that even a minor member of the royal family could possibly be dating a curvaceous half-dwarf, about as opposite to the tall glamourous elves as you could get. He ran his long finger down the paper clipped to a large stiff leaf the elves used as clipboards. With a curl of his lip, he crossed our names off and pointed to the large oval shaped portal behind him.

"No gryphons today?" Aloora asked hopefully, referring to the traditional elven mounts. Part lion, part eagle, the golden creatures had flown visitors down to the city last time we'd visited. I groaned internally. My friend clearly had a death wish and enjoyed all sorts of dangerous transportation. I did not.

"Not today," he replied haughtily, indicating the portal again.

Aloora shrugged and stepped through confidently. I glanced over the valley to the dark green forest. It was slightly unnerving that, with just one step, I'd be in the centre of the trees. I took a deep breath and followed my friend.

A strange sucking sensation surrounded me, accompanied by the feeling of falling sideways. Pale rainbows filled my vision and I closed my eyes against them. Flashes of forest entered my mind as the elven magic propelled me through the portal. Then it was over.

I stumbled out of the opalescent portal onto the moss-covered forest floor of Breconia. I put my hands on my knees and forced myself to breathe as the swimming feeling in my head slowly dissipated. Aloora was standing a few feet away, rocking on her heels with barely contained excitement at being back in the elven city.

We were in a large airy clearing with a stream babbling through the middle of it. Small rainbows reflected off the surface as it flowed over smooth pebbles. The red and brown tree trunks looked stark as they stretched upwards. The remains of autumn foliage that still clung to the treetops seemed more muted than I remembered when we had visited only a couple of months before.

Other leaves were already lining the forest floor, greyish brown in colour, reflecting the winter season. A flash of gold caught my eye as a gryphgeon flew overhead carrying a piece of paper in its claws. I shook my head, thoroughly out of my element among the lofty trees. The graceful elves that paced through the clearing were cloaked in dark colours and wore grim expressions. I nudged my friend and pointed in the direction that the elves seemed to be heading. We fell into step behind a group of willowy elves in shades of grey and silver and followed them along the broadest path.

We kept a respectful silence as we continued along. More groups of elves joined the pathway silently. Everything felt muted, even the usual elven glamour didn't feel as palpable as it had been last time we were here. Although I wasn't affected thanks to a charm I carried, I could still sense it thanks to the magical blood that ran through my own veins. Soft murmurs spread through the groups of elves as they spotted us walking alongside them, conspicuous as the smallest among them. Even their children were of a height with the two of us. I couldn't understand the words.

Most people shot us looks of interest but a significant number of the older elves' eyes were filled with distrust and hostility. I had a clear impression that we weren't welcome here. I walked nervously, tightening my grip on Bane, my ancestral axe, for reassurance in this alien place. Aloora was looking around brightly. Too brightly. I knew my friend could understand Elvish, among many other languages.

"What are they saying?" I whispered.

"Nothing." I gave her a look that told her I wasn't stupid, "Alright, fine. They're talking about you, being a dwarf, here in their city. It's not exactly an everyday occurrence you know and..."

"And?"

"Well they seem to know about your relationship with Lorandir and, it's not exactly...well...that is to say...they don't necessarily agree with it."

I nodded, blinking away the sudden hot tears that flamed in my eyes. I knew it was always going to be awkward dating an elf, but I somehow hadn't been prepared for the judgment that his entire race felt for me. It wasn't as if I could blend in, being about five foot nothing compared to their willowy heights. I forced myself to hold my head high as we carried on. There was such a thing as dwarven pride. I could almost feel Ironfist and my father's voices rebounding in my head not to lose face in front of the elves.

The path opened up into another clearing. My breath caught in my throat as my mind pulled away from introspection and onto the view of the central glade that contained the royal palace tree. Grey roots were exposed and lifted the trunk high above the forest floor. A turquoise stream wound around the huge tree, creating a moat around it.

More roots formed elegant bridges across the water. The leaves of the palace tree were true to its name – 'Evergreen'. The dark green foliage seemed too vibrant for the mood in the air. As we got closer to the palace, I noticed that some of the roots looked a little newer and more slender than the more established thick roots that supported the far side of the tree. A repair job.

A memory of a humongous dragon crashing through the root walls sprang into my mind. I shuddered involuntarily and gripped my axe more closely. I wouldn't forget there were dangerous magical creatures nearby.

Aloora elbowed me in the ribs and I realised that I'd stopped moving to stare and the elves were giving us disdainful looks as they flowed around us. Schiztz. More judgement. Great job Amethyst.

I stepped forward and began to cross the nearest bridge. I ran my hand over the smooth wood. It appeared carved but I knew that in fact elven magic had been used to mould the living tree into intricate bridges in a harmony of nature and magic. I felt the elven magic build as we got closer to the palace. As I stepped off the bridge, I felt a magical barrier form. I tried to step through but the barrier only solidified. I felt the familiar feeling of forest and moss in the elven magic. I pushed again and looked across at Aloora, panic starting to rise in my stomach. She was having trouble moving forward as well. We were stuck on the edge of the bridge in the middle of Breconia, unable to move.

Chapter 3

The elves had started to notice that we were stuck and a low murmuring began through the crowd. Some pushed past us and were able to leave the bridge unhindered. They shot us curious or hostile glances as they left us behind. I heard more mutterings I didn't understand, but I got the gist of the meaning, "Bloody dwarves," or something to that effect. I kept my gaze straight ahead and tried to avoid eye contact. Others decided to turn back and use other bridges to avoid the hold up. My heart sank as I saw a group of guards in the familiar grey and gold uniform heading in our direction. Aloora noticed them too and straightened her spine, preparing for confrontation.

The guards efficiently surrounded us and moved the crowd to other paths. My face flamed red as we were now firmly the centre of attention.

"Names," one of the guards asked sternly. He had three golden leaves pinned to one shoulder. I guessed that meant he was in charge here, some sort of captain or sergeant maybe.

"Aloora Dragonquest," my friend was confident and pointed her chin up in a challenge.

“Amethyst Haernson,” I mumbled. His nostrils flared at my Dwarfish surname.

“Do you know why you cannot cross the bridge?”

I shook my head mutely. Aloora narrowed her eyes, “Is it something to do with our magical signatures? We’re not elves but we have been invited.” She dug a fancy invitation card from a hidden pocket in her dress and waved it at the guard.

He dismissed it with a flick of his hand, “It is nothing to do with your species. It is because you are carrying weapons. Hand them over to me and you can enter.”

I blanched and held my axe tightly. The last time I had handed my axe over to an elf, I had been left defenceless when a dragon had stormed the palace. Aloora didn’t have the same attachment to her weapons and she lifted her dress to reveal a discreet crossbow strapped to her thigh. She handed it over and requested a receipt. The guard raised one eyebrow but dutifully signalled to one of the other soldiers, who scribbled something on a small round leaf and passed it to my friend. She inspected it. I knew she could understand the flowing cursive script and she nodded and took a step towards the palace.

The lead guard coughed, “All weapons, miss.”

Aloora turned guiltily and gave a depreciative laugh, “Silly me.” She bent down and extracted a small silver bladed knife from her boot. She flipped it carefully and handed it to him handle first. The captain continued to stare at her and she sighed before digging in her satchel for a final knife. I gaped at my friend. Since when had she become someone who carried so many weapons? She loved studying not fighting!

Again she studied the receipts she was given and this time she was able to step through the barrier.

The captain passed the weapons to one of the other guards. He turned to me and eyed my axe. He held his hand out. I shook my head. This was my ancestral axe, passed down to me by my father and through countless generations before that. I had already been parted from it too many times this year, by the mundane police force and the magical elves just a couple of months ago.

"It's cultural," I tried.

The captain narrowed his eyes, "Nevertheless…"

I shook my head again and took a step back as I thought about what to do. I could insist on keeping the axe and miss the ceremony. That idea sounded appealing. Guiltily, my thoughts turned to Lorandir. The elf who was meant to be my partner and who had asked me to attend for moral support as they commemorated his uncle. Schiztz. I knew what my choice would be. I couldn't let Lorandir down. With a final squeeze of the axe's shaft, I handed Bane over to the elf. One of the other elves handed me a rounded leaf with flowing Elvish script scrawled over it. I tucked it into my corset top, closed my eyes and followed Aloora.

"Amethyst! I heard you were here!" My elf strode across the clearing to meet us. I smiled up at him weakly as he pulled me into a hug. He noticed my mood and pulled back, searching my eyes with his green gaze. Frowning, he took in the guards still standing on the bridge and my dwarven axe standing out obviously against their elven uniforms, "What's this then?"

The captain gave an awkward salute, "Fulfilling our orders, sir! No weapons allowed near the Evergreen palace, sir!" His tone had changed from menacing to enthusiastically trying to impress a member of the royal family. I hadn't realised how much respect Lorandir carried here, he had told me he was a minor member of royalty. Interesting. I had assumed his royal status just got him invited to some swanky parties, I had obviously misunderstood how much weight whatever title he had carried.

"Nonsense. Amethyst is my guest and friend to the dwarven ambassador and that is a dwarven battle axe, of great historic importance. If the dwarves knew we were so disrespectful of their culture, I shudder to think of the repercussions."

The captain blanched slightly. Relations between the two races were never easy but some headway had been made when Ironfist had been allowed to escort me to the Equinox Ball as dwarven ambassador. "Just carrying out orders, sir."

"No doubt and I will be sure to tell your superior how dutifully you did so. As for these ladies, they are under my care and I will take full responsibility for them and their weapons while they are within the palace grounds. Now, please return their possessions."

I wasn't sure I liked the way his voice changed subtly as if he was used to being obeyed. Bloody haughty elves. The thought entered my head before I could stop it. I flushed, embarrassed by my own mind. Lorandir wasn't like that. He was clearly playing a part to get my axe back. One of the guards returned the axe to my hands and I caressed the handle lovingly, as if it had been more than just minutes since it had last been in my grasp. I stood on my tiptoes to give Lorandir a quick kiss on the cheek.

"Thank you," I murmured.

He looked amused. Elves could never understand the attachment dwarves had to their weapons, but he knew it was important to me. My earlier treacherous thoughts about elves disappeared as he waved his hands in a complicated pattern towards the palace. I felt rather than saw the magic barrier lift temporarily. He held my hand and we stepped off the bridge. He escorted us towards the palace tree and then stopped.

"You know, you really didn't need to bring your axe today."

I frowned at him, "You should know I did after what happened the last time we were here."

"I can protect you against any threats."

"Like the chimera or the dragon?" I saw him wince at my words. A reminder of some of the dangers we had faced last time we were in Breconia. It was a low blow but I didn't want him to feel like he had to protect me. I was capable of protecting myself, as long as I had my axe.

"As you wish. At least let me top up the invisibility enchantment on it, that way only those closest to you will see it." I nodded and allowed him to cast the spell over the axe. Again the intoxicating signature of his magic flowed around me. I allowed myself to close my eyes and breathe it in. He finished and linked my arm through his, "There are still a couple of hours before the ceremony, shall I show you to your rooms?"

Aloora nodded in agreement, “Then I want to check out the library.”

“Of course, I am sure that Shesalva is looking forward to seeing you again.”

I smiled as Aloora tried to look cool at the mention of the slender, red-headed elf who had taken charge of her during our last visit. Then I blanched as we headed towards the steps encircling the palace with their twining ivy handrails. Lorandir noticed my discomfort and led us past the steps to a portal. I sighed with relief that I didn’t have to scale the tall tree. We stepped through and once the rainbows had cleared from my vision, I could see Aloora being shown to the same room she had stayed in before. I studied the carvings of various treaty signings decorating the walls and wandered down the hallway to my previous room while the elf ensured she was settled in. Once he was assured that she could remember the way to the library and wouldn’t be late for the ceremony, he slid the large leaf door shut and walked towards me.

“Am I staying in here again?” I pointed towards the door that I thought led to the same room I had stayed in before.

“You could…but it would be my pleasure to show you my own chambers.”

My heart started beating faster. I nodded and tried to stop myself turning pink with pleasure. Somehow I had assumed he would be cold and distant back in his home city and supporting his cousin’s new kingship. He smiled and kissed the back of my hand. I felt my stomach flutter as his warm lips brushed my skin.

He smiled again and tucked my hand into the crook of his arm as he led the way back to the shimmering portal. He kept his opposite hand over mine, rubbing his thumb over the spot where he had kissed me. My insides continued to flutter as we stepped into the portal. This time I nearly did fall as we staggered out. I leant against Lorandir, trying to get my bearings as my head cleared from the dizziness of portal travel.

We were in another room inside the palace. This one had an oak leaf border carved into the wall. The border curved around a relief of a large oak tree growing from a single smooth acorn. The branches and leaves seemed to form some sort of writing.

"What is that?"

Lorandir's gaze turned thoughtful, "It is my family's crest. The motto is worked into the design: Nordo melehta iesta erde nipa." At my questioning look, he translated, "Mighty oaks start from small seeds. It reminds us that everything has power, even the tiny acorn."

"It's different to the royal crest." The royal crest was a tree with a golden crown looped around the trunk. I guessed it was meant to represent the Evergreen palace. It certainly didn't look like an oak tree.

His face became clouded and I regretted speaking my thoughts aloud. "Yes, it is. A legacy of many years ago. The royal family has always been supported by a council of three. Three reflects the trinity of nature and the balance of things. The idea is that the King or Queen does not rule alone and is provided with good advice…although it does not protect from all bad decisions." He paused, reflecting on his Uncle's decision to steal a dragon egg and become the first dragon rider in millennia. The decision that had ultimately led to his demise.

I squeezed his hand gently, trying to reassure him. He squeezed back and continued his story, "One of my ancestors was annoyed that the kingship was hereditary rather than going to the best person for the role. Best meaning him in that case. He was also overlooked for the council many thousand of years ago; his youth was held against him.

"The legend is that the Queen at the time is supposed to have said those words to him as reassurance that his time would come. In a petty or strong move depending on which side of the family you are on, he took those words to heart and created a separate crest to remind everyone that even those that look weak have the potential for great power."

"What happened to him?"

"After a couple of centuries of whispering and negotiating, he was able to convince the High Council that the king must be selected by the people to cement his rule. In this way, if any future rulers are suspected of not having the best elven interests at heart, they can be prevented from gaining power. I believe he hoped that he may have been chosen, but the elves of the time wholeheartedly endorsed the incumbent Queen."

I let out a low whistle, "So, have any future kings or queens been prevented from taking the throne?"

"Not to date," his face darkened and his symmetrical eyebrows pulled together in a frown, "but there is talk about Morthimas and a worry that his father has corrupted him. This ceremony today is a memorial for King Lireath who had many years of good rule until…the dragon. But it should also be the ceremony to crown my cousin. That is why we have waited so long since my Uncle passed on: there have been many discussions about what should be done."

"But they're going to crown Morthimas right?"

Lorandir shook his head, "I hope so." He turned to me and seemed to suddenly realise that I was still carrying my overnight bag and my axe, "Let's get you to our room."

I smiled slightly as he said 'our'. It still amazed me that we, two seemingly different people, worlds away from each other were together. I looked around the room so he didn't think I was stupid for grinning at nothing and then frowned. The chamber we were standing in was a dead end. The portal was still there, glowing a pale opal colour that lit up the greyish wood of the tree but there were none of the sliding doors formed from massive leaves that there had been in the guest chambers.

"I can't see a door."

Lorandir smiled and stepped forward to the carved tree. He put a hand against the acorn and I felt his magic flow in a sensation of warm honey and dark chocolate. The tree moved apart until there was a large enough gap for us to pass through unhindered. I blinked and tried to act as though finding secret doors in palaces was a perfectly everyday occurrence. He bowed me through into his private quarters.

The room was large, nearly as large as the flat I shared with Aloora and Marco. Wooden furniture was arranged to look cosy with a large curved seating area to one side. A bookshelf was sunk into another part of the tree, filled with leather bound books that oozed knowledge. There was even a space that looked like it could be a kitchen, with curved cupboards and a polished wooden side.

Luxurious throws and huge cushions were strewn over the chairs in natural greens that enhanced the feel of nature in the room. I walked over to the seating area and ran my hand over a throw. It was soft to touch and I wanted to wrap myself up in it.

“Do you like it?” Lorandir sounded nervous as he stayed by the door while I explored.

“It’s beautiful, but…wasn’t there a bed here last time?” I eyed the carved seating area, it didn’t look like the bedroom I’d been taken to after being almost killed by a dragon a couple of months ago. My memory of the whole thing was hazy but there had definitely been a bed.

The elf laughed, a melodious sound that I loved hearing, “The bedroom is up there.” He gestured to the stairs that curved upwards at the back of the room.

Surprisingly, there was a handrail that accompanied the steps. I walked closer and noted the intertwining oak leaves that patterned the rail. At the top of the stairs was a familiar sliding leaf door in a dark green colour that made the golden veins stand out prominently. I moved it to one side and stepped in.

Grey light filled the room from a large window on the opposite side, illuminating the huge bed. I leant my axe against the wall and dumped my bag in the alcove where Lorandir’s own clothes were hanging. A mixture of modern jeans and t-shirts and floor-length elven robes. Having relieved myself of my things, I sat on the bed. It sagged slightly under my weight and I lay back, allowing my legs to dangle off the edge. Lorandir smiled down at me.

"Come join me?" I suggested.

He shook his head regretfully, "I should be with Morthimas, he is already anxious about today."

I nodded curtly.

"Will you be alright here? I will return before the ceremony to escort you…or you can wander the city?"

I couldn't imagine anything worse than wandering the city alone and having elegant elves stare at the stocky half-dwarf. "I'll stay here. I'm sure I can find a book to read or take a bath or something."

Lorandir looked dubious, torn between his desire to be with me and the need to support his cousin and lifelong friend.

"Go on, shoo!" I sat up and made a shoo-ing motion with my hand to accompany the words, "I'll be fine. If you're feeling that guilty, you can make it up to me later…"

He gave me a lingering kiss, "It's a deal…"

He walked to the door then looked back hesitantly. I repeated the shoo-ing gesture and he shook his head and left. I was tempted to have a bath in the amazing bathrooms they had here but didn't want my make-up to run, I could never remember if my non-brand mascara was waterproof. I thought about trying to meet up with Aloora but knowing the gnome, she'd already be in the library either studying or trying to get close to the attractive librarian. Instead, I called Marco. He answered immediately and I grinned as his familiar handsome face filled my screen.

"'Allo, 'ow are the elves?"

"You know elves…" I shrugged. He nodded. He knew one elf at least. He and Lorandir got on so well, sometimes people mistook them for a couple. "How's Errol doing?"

Marco tilted the phone so I could see my small red wyrm curled up on a fire-proof blanket next to him. His head perked up at my voice and he stared at the phone. Marco gave him a friendly rub behind his wing joints.

"'E is doing well. 'E 'as been 'elping me strip paint from a table. 'Is flames are very useful sometimes." The camera flicked so I could see the table. There was a paint scraper lying on top of it and the remaining yellow paint looked charred. I wondered where the table was going to go in our apartment.

Aloora had already bought a schiztz ton of flat pack furniture just after we moved into our new place in Cardiff Bay. I decided to keep the peace and not mention it; their tastes were very different.

"Good, good. I'm glad you're getting along."

"I 'ad to disconnect the fire alarm but 'e is 'appy and 'e enjoys my programmes." That last remark sounded pointed. His home makeover shows were easy to watch but the formula got repetitive and I couldn't really get into the soap operas he liked either.

"Great, that's really good…well we'll be back tomorrow so see you soon."

"'Ave fun!"

"Marco! We're here for a funeral!"

He hung up before he heard my admonishment.

Part of me wished I was curled up next to them in my own home. I'd even suffer through the latest illogical drama in whichever soap opera was on tonight. Instead I was on my own here, in danger of wallowing in self-pity.

With a sigh, I heaved myself off the soft bed and went downstairs to find a book. I perused the bookshelf and my heart sank. Of course all the books were in Elvish. I picked one at random and flicked through. Indecipherable Elvish script curled across the page. I turned to the centre pages and found some printed pictures. All the figures had crowns so I guessed they were Kings and Queens of old, but the elven robes they were wearing looked so similar to what they continued to wear for formal events that it was impossible to tell when they had ruled. I closed the book and replaced it on the shelf.

A splash of bright colour caught my eye and I reached up to pull down a book that looked out of place. I couldn't stop the smile spreading across my face when I saw it was by my favourite fantasy author. So Lorandir had listened to me and was reading one of my favourite books. That elf made my heart melt. I curled up on the carved sofa against the soft cushions and began to read. I was about twenty pages in when a knock on the door made me jump.

Chapter 4

I stood up and walked over to where the door had been. I stared at the wood, now magically sealed again. Only a thin seam marked where the opening would appear. The knock sounded persistently. I leant my ear against the door.

"Hello?"

"Oh, good morning Amethyst. Can you get Lorandir? It's me, Morty."

Schiztz. Prince Morthimas was at the door. "Er, he's not here."

I heard a stream of Elvish from the other side. I guessed he was swearing. "Can I come in anyway? I need a few minutes away from them."

"Of course," I guessed Lorandir would be fine for his private quarters to be a sanctuary for his friend. I took a step back and glared at the door. "Open up tree!" Nothing happened.

There was a pause before Morthimas spoke again, "What did you just say?"

"Er, I was asking the tree to open the door, but it, er…didn't work. Can you open it from that side?"

“It’s aligned to Lorandir’s magical signature, but you should be able to open it from the inside. Try asking it in Elvish.”

I blinked at the tree trying to remember the words Lorandir had used. My mind drew a blank. As if he could read my discomfort, Morthimas provided the words for me. I repeated them as best as I could. After the third try, the tree opened the door. I had no connection to the living tree but I patted the wood softly and whispered a thank you to the tree as the prince strode in and stretched himself out on the wooden sofa. He covered his eyes with his hands and let out a groan.

I stood there wondering what to do awkwardly, “Er, can I get you something to drink?”

“Tea please,” Morthimas kept his hands over his face.

I walked over to the area I had assumed was a kitchen and began opening cupboards. I found mugs, carved from different types of wood. Obviously. There was a small chest made of intricate interlocking pieces of different coloured wood. I ran my hands over the smooth surface with wonder. The craftsmanship was exquisite. I opened it reverently and found different bags of tea. A faint floral scent wafted towards me. I selected two at random and plonked them into two large mugs. There was a teapot, which I ignored, but no kettle. I spotted the wooden tap spouting discreetly from the wall and turned it on. Maybe the tap gave out hot water directly like in the bathrooms, where steaming hot water flowed on demand. Cool, crystal-clear spring water flowed into the mugs. Not hot water then. I left the teabags in the mugs to brew as best they could in the cold water and took them over to where the prince was lying on the comfy cushions. He heard me approaching and forced himself to a seating position. I handed him one of the cups. He sniffed delicately.

"What is this?"

"Er, tea."

"Why is the teabag in the cup?"

"So it can brew."

He considered this with the sort of look I got when processing the words vegan chocolate. He decided to stop thinking and took a sip before making a face, "It's cold."

"I couldn't find a kettle."

He blinked at me, "We don't have kettles, we use magic to warm the teapot. Maybe I'd better make the tea."

I followed him to the kitchen area. He seemed happier now he had some sort of purpose and I was happy to have a hot drink. I watched as he took his time choosing a bag of tea leaves.

"Each of our teas is specially blended to fit the occasion or our mood. Normally I'd choose loose leaves but Lorandir prefers the ready bagged stuff." He picked out two of the bags and showed them to me. They looked exactly the same as the other bags in the chest, "This is a mint blend. It helps to calm the mind and body, allowing us to focus."

He placed the tea bags into the teapot and closed his eyes. I felt the power begin to flow from him into the pot, heating it. "And now we wait for it to brew."

I nodded, still feeling awkward, "Do you need to be calmed?"

“What?” His green eyes, so like his cousin’s, were sharp and wary as he snapped his gaze away from the teapot towards my face.

“I mean, you said mint tea is calming…are you anxious? Do you need to be calmed?”

He let out a sigh and his shoulders slumped slightly, “I had wanted to talk to Lorandir, he always knows what to say to me but I suppose I can confide in you. It’s not like you’re close to anyone here.” His words made me feel suddenly very alone in this unfamiliar place. “But yes, I do need to be calmed. Now that my claim to the throne has been accepted, something that the Council debated endlessly by the way, it feels like everyone is waiting for me to mess up, just because my father…well…because he was an idiot frankly. He believed his council when they whispered words about dragon riders and power and he was stupid enough to believe he could do it.

“Now half the elves in this country want me to step aside, and I’ve half a mind to do it, but what would that do? Leave a vacuum for someone else to fill and make us more divided, more susceptible to evil influences and worse off than before. So what should I do? Step up and have everyone suspicious of me because of my father or step aside and have everyone hate me for weakening our people?”

It was a rhetorical question, but I couldn’t stop the swearword that left my lips, “Dzrak, and I thought my life was complicated.”

"How is your life complicated?" There was genuine curiosity in his voice but also a slight undercurrent that pissed me off.

"Just because I'm not about to become King for a bunch of people who mistrust me doesn't mean my life isn't complex. I'm a half-dwarf dating a dzraking elf. No one's particularly happy about that, except Mum maybe…" I shook my head, "Sorry, I'm not helping."

A slow smile spread across his face, "You are right, we both have difficult paths to tread." He turned and poured the tea thoughtfully. The aroma of mint filled the space. He handed me a mug. "To life's challenges." He raised his mug to mine. I chinked the wood together with a hearty clunk.

"Cheers to that." We both took long drinks. "So, have you decided what you're going to do?"

"No," he met my eyes again, "what would you do if you were me?"

I spluttered on my tea. I was completely unqualified to be giving out life advice to royalty, "Er, I don't know…it's your life, you have to be comfortable with your own choices. So, these people who are suspicious of you, do they know you?"

"Not really."

"Do you know them?"

His lips lifted in a half smile, "Not all of them."

"So, if you become King, you might end up impressing them?"

"Maybe."

"Or if you don't know them and it doesn't matter what they think, you could leave Breconia and kingship behind and never worry about it again."

"Don't tempt me. Where would I go?"

"Wherever you wanted! But I imagine you could stay at Lorandir's place in Cardiff Bay for starters."

He took another drink, considering. His brows were furrowed together in a frown.

"But I don't think you want to leave."

"No?" he raised an eyebrow at me.

I shook my head, "If you wanted to leave, you'd have jumped at the chance. I think you care too much about your people. And that's why you're going to be a great leader."

He inclined his head to me and raised his mug again, "Well cheers to that."

"You know, if we were both dwarves, we'd be drinking something alcoholic right now…"

He smiled again, "I'd better leave that until after the ceremony!"

"It's a date."

Lorandir strode into the room looking worried. His eyes took in the both of us leaning on the cupboards and sipping tea, "Thank goodness, here you are! I've been looking everywhere for you!" He practically ran over and hugged his cousin, then he pushed back and looked between us, "Wait what was that about a date?"

I smiled back, savouring the moment that the inhumanly attractive elf was jealous that I might be about to date his cousin. Morthimas spoiled it by laughing heartily and reassuring him, “Nothing like that. Amethyst’s been helping me decide what to do so I owe her a drink. I can see why you like her.”

I raised my teacup with a tilt of my head. Lorandir narrowed his eyes at me but didn’t push it. Instead he poured himself a cup of the fragrant mint tea and gestured to the seating area. I curled up at the end of the sofa nearest the wall, forming a small nest of cushions around me.

“So, what did you decide Morty?”

“Well thanks to your better half,” the prince nodded at me and I gave him an encouraging smile, “I have decided to accept the crown.”

“Thank goodness! I knew you’d come to your senses.”

“Well we both know you’d be rubbish at ruling!”

“What?!” I spat out my tea, causing droplets to fall onto the silken cushion. I rubbed at it with the sleeve of my cardigan. Both elves started laughing.

“Don’t worry, Lorandir wouldn’t be chosen if I wasn’t King.”

“Good, but, I mean why not?” I was glad there wouldn’t be any more complications right now but a bit perturbed that Morthimas so easily discounted my other half.

“Well, I mean…he wouldn’t…”

“I wouldn’t be a suitable choice, that’s all. We should really get you ready for the ceremony, your highness.”

I narrowed my eyes. The atmosphere in the room had gone from amiable to tense too fast and the elves were exchanging glances and getting up too hastily. I decided not to press it…for now.

“I’ll come too,” I decided and stood with them, “just let me get my bag.” I ran upstairs and took a small clutch bag from my backpack. Ironfist, member of the Dwarven High Council and now ambassador to the elves, had fashioned the chain into a holster for my axe. I slotted it in and walked downstairs more carefully, now slightly unbalanced by the weight of Bane on one side. I could almost hear Lorandir’s groan as he spotted my weapon, but to his credit he did his best to not moan aloud. The prince’s eyes lighted on my axe and stared.

“Traditionally, weapons are not carried at a memorial or crowning ceremony…” Morthimas started.

I raised my chin in defiance, but Lorandir spoke before I could. He sounded weary and put upon as he put a hand on his cousin’s arm, “Don’t, just don’t. Trust me on this!”

I flashed him a dazzling smile as I walked to his side and gave him a quick kiss. That was my elf. Morthimas looked less sure so Lorandir added, “I will take full responsibility for Amethyst while she is here.”

The prince seemed dubious but let it go. He led the way out of the chambers and through the portal. I forced myself to keep moving as I left the portal. Trees whirled across my eyes in double vision before I acclimatised and realised we were on the forest floor outside the Evergreen Palace. A small group of elves began heading our way. Lorandir and Morthimas tensed beside me. This couldn’t be good.

Chapter 5

I tried not to stare, but several of the elves had a greyish pallor instead of the golden tans I had grown used to seeing in Breconia. The tallest elf bowed slightly, his dark hair flopping over his forehead. Morthimas inclined his head in greeting.

"Commander Mordred."

The grey-skinned elf smiled, revealing slightly pointed teeth, "Your highness, or should that be almost highness?"

The future King stiffened, "The coronation is a formality, as I'm sure you're aware. And I'm surprised to see you here. It must have been centuries since the dark elves last graced us with their presence."

"I wouldn't have missed a coronation, such a rare event for our people. We were once not so very different, and I like to honour that memory. Besides, it's always so exciting, you never know who you might meet at these things." His dark eyes swept over me, resting on my chest and he raised an eyebrow. I glared back at him and tried to ignore my cheeks heating. "Is that an Avalonian crystal? It's been so long since I've seen such a gem. May I?"

I felt a dark wave of strange glamour wash over me in a sickly-sweet wave. I had a sudden urge to do exactly what he wanted and hand over my necklace. My hand reached for the jewel but as my fingers brushed it, I stopped. What was I thinking? This was my namesake crystal, a gift from Avalon if Madam Mim, the powerful sorceress, was to be believed.

Mordred frowned at my reticence. His hand snaked out towards my neck. I stepped backwards, clutching the amethyst tighter as Lorandir grabbed his wrist, stopping him from touching me.

He withdrew his arm and bowed again, "My apologies. Please forgive my rudeness."

I nodded curtly. I didn't need to start any diplomatic incidents today. But his dark eyes met mine with a strange hunger that I couldn't place. We stood in awkward silence before one of the elves – an older man with long white hair and dazzling blue eyes – stepped towards Morthimas.

"My lord, we should discuss details of the trade treaty with the humans. They are requesting more magic users to protect their parliament buildings and a marriage alliance with their own royal family to try to stop the advancement of anti-magic feeling."

Morthimas shot us a pleading look over the older elf's head.

Lorandir interrupted the elf's next sentence, "My apologies Councillor, but the King must prepare himself."

"Of course, your majesty," the group of elves all bowed their heads as Lorandir hastily ushered both the Prince and me inside the palace tree and up smooth wooden steps before the oncoming group made it to where we were standing. I vaguely recognised the direction we were being pushed in, Lorandir's hand firmly in mine, forcing me to stay with them. I was almost running to keep up with the elves' long legs as we spiralled up the tree, and then finally, Lorandir opened a door and motioned me and Prince Morthimas inside.

Green light flooded the simple room. A dark shape wearing a long elven robe embroidered in gold and green stood to one side. Movement behind it caught my eye and I stepped forward, starting to slip Bane from its holster before my brain caught up with my eyes. The figure was a costume dummy, clothed in presumably the elven equivalent of robes of state. The movement was us entering the room, reflected in a large mirror. This was a dressing room.

"Thank you, I thought I was going to have to talk more politics," Morthimas sunk onto a pile of rich cushions on the floor.

Lorandir shrugged, "You don't have long before the ceremony, then you'll have to talk politics with everybody."

"You're not helping!"

My elf grinned and I covered my hand to hide my own smile. Thank goodness I wasn't involved with politics. The Prince's eyes narrowed at his friend, "You think this is funny. Trust me, my problems will be nothing compared to yours…" he stopped abruptly and turned away. I had caught the warning glance in Lorandir's eyes though.

So our relationship was now a problem? Schiztz. I turned away and rested my palm on my ancestral axe to calm myself. There was too much wood and nature here, I wanted to feel the hard coolness of my natural element: metal. Bane glowed under my touch, picking up some of my emotions. I felt the elf's hand on my shoulder. I forced myself to be calm, "Aren't you meant to be getting ready for a ceremony? I'll leave you to it."

"I'd rather you stayed. I don't want you to be alone here."

"Hey, don't even worry about it. I'm a big girl, I can take care of myself," I turned so my axe was more prominent.

"I still really don't think you should have…"

Lorandir hissed something in Elvish and the Prince shut up with a shrug.

"Don't worry, I won't use it unless I have to. See you at the ceremony."

Lorandir bent his head to brush my forehead with his lips. I allowed myself to lean against him before I pulled away and opened the door.

I shut it and rested against the smooth wood for a moment. Dzrak. Things were complicated. I knew that. But problems? I hadn't really thought this through. I began to descend the spiralling steps slowly. My boots thudded against the wood. I winced at the noise. It seemed like the whole forest was quiet and I was out of my depth here. Treading more softly, I continued along, my only thought to get to the bottom of the dzraking palace and find a spot at the back of the hall, safely tucked away from disapproving glares.

Pairs of guards passed me on the way down but apart from questioning looks and narrowed eyes, they left me be. One benefit of dating a member of the royal family, I supposed.

It took an age to reach the bottom of the stairs but finally my feet were on the springy moss of the forest floor again. Deep in my spiralling thoughts, I almost ran into the dark elf delegation who were murmuring with the white-haired councillor. They stopped talking and stared at me. I bobbed in something between a curtsey and a bow then moved on before they could say anything to me. As I walked away, I thought I heard the word “Avalon” murmured by one of his retinue before Mordred cut them off.

I forced myself not to turn. I had been gifted the amethyst at my neck without realising it came from Avalon and I wasn’t about to let some creepy dark elf have something that I considered so pure. I reached into my bag to touch the anti-glamour charm I knew was in there. Immediately I felt surer of myself and I carried on with a more purposeful stride.

I headed for the exposed silvery roots that lifted the palace away from the ground and provided a covered space for the elves. I slunk between two large roots and was immediately struck by the openness of the space.

For the Equinox Ball, the elven architects had closed the openings between the roots and rich tapestries had covered the walls. Now there was a large grey tapestry hanging behind a dais containing a throne. The royal crest was woven into it in shining gold and dark green. Glowing orbs of light were floating around the large space, lighting it in tones of soft candlelight, giving the space a cathedral-like feel.

Seats formed from logs were lined in rows of semi circles in front of the dais, with a break in the centre to allow someone to walk up the middle. A small number of seats were already occupied by elves whispering together. Their flowing robes were in various shades of grey or dark browns or greens. All natural colours. I tugged my cardigan closer around myself, wishing I hadn't worn black. Apparently it was the wrong choice for an elven funeral or memorial. I sat down on one of the seats right at the back, at one of the far ends. I would make sure I was as inconspicuous as possible.

I was aware of eyes on me and decided to use the tried and tested technique of ignoring everyone by staring at my phone. I pulled it out and texted Aloora to let her know where I was and to tell her to hurry up. Then I scrolled through social media. I managed to lose myself in an online debate over whether or not there were bees in the Lord of the Rings when I felt someone touch my elbow. I looked up and straight into the light blue eyes of an elf. She spoke to me in low, rapid Elvish and gestured towards the front of the room with her elegant hand.

"Er…" I felt my face turning red as I had no idea what she had said. I followed the direction of her hand and noticed that while I had been engrossed in the reasons why bees had or hadn't existed in Middle Earth, the room was now nearly full. Apart from the seat next to me, which they had avoided like I had some sort of disease. Elves were murmuring to each other softly in muted tones. The elf by my side repeated her missive slower and more loudly.

Like that was going to help me to understand her. It had an effect on the elves around me though, who began turning to see why one of their people was speaking so loudly. I wanted to sink into the ground with embarrassment as they all began turning towards me, some of their beautiful faces were curious, others were hostile and I think I caught disdain from a few of the older elves with visibly white hair. I looked around helplessly and spotted the one other speck of black in the sea of more natural mourning colours. Aloora. I met her eyes and tried to signal that I was in trouble.

She mouthed something at me and patted a seat next to her. Was I meant to go to her? I shrugged and stood. I saw the gnome roll her eyes and then she was forcing her way through the row of seats to the centre aisle, which she strode down and around the back until she was beside me. The tall elf repeated her words and Aloora replied in rapid fluent Elvish. The elf seemed satisfied with the answer and moved off to stand by the wall. I followed her with my eyes as she took out one of the leaf clipboards and scribbled something on it.

My friend tugged me upright, "You're meant to be sitting with the delegation from the Magical Liaison Office. With me. What were you thinking? Didn't you see the seating chart on the way in?"

"Seating chart? I just came in through one of the gaps in the wall."

I couldn't see her face as she was propelling me towards our seats but I had been friends with her long enough to know when Aloora was rolling her eyes, "I've been trying to catch your attention. What were you doing on your phone?!"

"Er, I was on a forum…do you think there were bees in Lord of the Rings?"

Aloora stopped for a moment before continuing her forward momentum. At our designated row, she apologised as we sidestepped past long-legged elves to take our seats. There were murmurs of disapproval as we edged along. I tried to copy Aloora's words of apology as we went, especially after I trod on someone's foot.

I turned to say sorry face to face and managed to elbow the elf in front of me in the back of the head. As I turned again, my axe hit the first elf's knee. My face flaming red, I muttered what I hoped was an apology as my friend tugged me into my seat. I buried my face in my hands just after I saw the first elf rubbing his foot and giving me an evil glare. Schiztz. I don't think that could have gone any worse. Then I heard my name.

I looked up and met Lorandir's gaze. So he had seen everything, and there was me thinking this couldn't have gone any worse. He gestured for me to come to him. Aloora slipped my bag off my shoulder and nudged me over. I diplomatically decided to go the other way than I had come. I didn't think I could face sore foot again and he was still looking at me like he could turn me into a toad with his mind. Without the bulk of my axe, I managed to make it across the row without injuring anyone. Lorandir had already walked around with an easy grace that I envied.

"I am sorry I can't sit with you during the ceremony. I have to sit with my family." Schiztz. Of course his family would be here, I just hadn't appreciated that I might be in the same room as them. I glanced over to where two stately elves were sitting, watching us blankly. I gave them a nervous smile and a half wave. Their expressions didn't change. "I have something for you…"

I blanched as I looked down to his hand, which was now holding a small jewellery box. Being elven, it was covered with leaves rather than velvet or leather, although somehow they looked polished. "Er…I'm not sure…"

He looked amused as he opened it to reveal a small wooden charm carved into the shape of a delicate tree, "It will help you understand the ceremony." He took it out of the leaf box and pressed it into my hand while leaning forward intimately. "Thank you for being here," he whispered in my ear. It took me a second to realise that it was Elvish he was speaking and I understood him perfectly.

"Thank you," I murmured back. He kissed my cheek and returned to his seat. I looked around the room. If it wasn't obvious before, now everyone here knew that one of their royal family was dating a half-dwarf. From some of the dark looks I was getting, I didn't think that was a good thing. I tiptoed my way back to Aloora's side and sat down. I opened my palm and showed her the small charm. She nodded as if she'd expect nothing less. I unclipped the chain holding my amethyst necklace in place and slipped the charm onto it.

I had no idea if it had to be touching my skin to work but I wasn't taking any chances. I wouldn't embarrass myself or Lorandir again today. Instantly I was able to understand the people speaking around me. They were still talking in hushed tones so I couldn't make out everything, but I caught the gist enough to make my ears heat.

"A dwarf here! I never thought I'd live to see the day."

"…no right to be here…"

“And did you see her accosting the Prince? Such displays of affection!”

“How is Morthimas going to rule if he can’t even control his cousin?”

“There were mead halls,” Aloora’s voice interrupted my eavesdropping.

“What?”

“In Lord of the Rings. The Rohirrim had mead halls. Mead is from honey so there must be bees in Middle Earth, even if Tolkien doesn’t directly mention them. Now make sure your phone is on silent, please!”

Huh. I couldn’t fault her logic. In a slightly better mood, I turned off my phone just as a mournful blast sounded from an elven horn. The ceremony had begun.

Chapter 6

A reverent hush fell over the crowded room. Then everyone stood. I followed suit, straining to see between the tall elves. There was no way I'd be able to look over them. Among all the formal elven robes, I thought I caught sight of one made from dark coloured tweed. The robe disappeared from my view as the elves moved and I forgot about it as we all turned towards the main entrance and looked down the middle aisle.

A golden robe was carried high by four tall elves in familiar grey and gold uniforms. This was followed by another soldier, a higher rank judging by the amount of gold woven through his uniform, carrying a portrait of King Lireath painted expertly onto smooth bark. I studied the features through a gap in the crowd as it passed us. It looked like a good likeness from what I could remember, although the artist had missed out the craziness I had seen in his eyes when he had tried to snatch the dragon's egg from me. The robe was laid out on the floor in front of the dais and I noticed several elves lift two fingers to their foreheads in some sort of sign of respect. Others turned their faces away. Interesting.

The portrait was placed gently onto a wooden stand I hadn't noticed at the head of the robe.

I guess that garment was meant to represent the old King. I was hazy on what had happened to his body after I had been knocked out the last time I was here, but I was also a complete novice at elven funerals so maybe this was normal. My thoughts drifted to a distant relative's funeral I'd had to attend a few years ago. There had been bonfires, feasting and fighting. A typical dwarven funeral and about as far from this staid elven ceremony as you could get.

I was pulled back to the present as everyone turned to watch two guards process down the aisle. They were carrying an absurdly large dark green cushion, trimmed with more gold. I recognised the royal crest as it caught the light, flashing gold under the floating magical orbs that lit the chamber. Atop the cushion was a large crown. I appraised it as it went past us. Simple design, nicely worked. No visible joins. Gold. Obviously. It looked elf-made but without touching it I couldn't tell for sure.

Elves weren't known for their metalwork; they preferred to work with living materials like wood but when they did, I had to acknowledge that they were good. And the rarity made any elven metalwork expensive. I sensed something in the metal; a faint niggle tugging at my mind. An enchantment. I nodded appreciatively. Some artefacts had magic worked into them to strengthen the wearer or instil them with wisdom or whatever. I guessed it was something like that. The guards took up position on the dais, still holding the cushion.

Prince Morthimas paced solemnly and alone past us all. The golden robe he was wearing made him look more regal than I had seen him, more distant. Then I saw that his eyes were fixed straight ahead. I thought he looked nervous and tried to give him an encouraging smile, not that he could see me behind all the six foot plus elves. He reached the dais and sat on the vacant throne, his face grim. Everyone sat a millisecond after Morthimas' bottom touched the throne. I copied them, not wanting to stand out for any reason.

An elf in the front row stood. He was wearing a white robe and had long, perfectly straight white hair with two small plaits braided either side of his face, trimmed with wooden beads. He took slow steps up to the dais and stood almost directly in front of Morthimas. He closed his eyes and touched two fingers to his forehead before raising his arms and addressing us all.

"Today is a sad day for elf-kind. We gather to commemorate our beloved King Lireath, first of his name." There was a sharp intake of breath from the majority of the crowd at the word beloved. "He ruled over us for two hundred and three short years, steering us through many changes in this world with the guidance of his wise Council." I caught Morthimas' eyes narrow at that statement. This was starting to feel much more hostile. "It is our way to bury our dead that they may nurture our forest and return to the earth. We are unable to do this today, so instead we honour the man he was and his legacy of peace between the nations."

I had to stop myself from scoffing at that. He had stolen a dragon egg to try to become a dragon rider and claim more power. They were unable to bury him because he had been vapourised by a stream of dragon poison.

"He leaves behind his Queen and his son, Prince Morthimas, who mourn him deeply. It is the way of nature that all seasons must change and so I now turn to our new King." Morthimas stood and moved forward. Both elves turned to face each other.

"Morthimas, son of Lireath, do you promise to be just and wise as befits our ruler?"

"I do."

"Will you listen to others before you speak as befits our ruler?"

"I will."

"Will you uphold our laws and honour our land as befits our ruler?"

"I will."

"Do you accept the burden to rule?"

"I do."

The older elf pulled Morthimas towards him and they touched their foreheads together. Both turned towards the seated crowd.

"Morthimas accepts the burden of ruler of the elves. Do you here today now accept him in turn?"

There was a moment of tense silence. Morthimas' jaw clenched. This was the moment he had been worried about, that he wouldn't be accepted. The front row stood. I saw the previous Queen, tears glistening in her eyes. Lorandir and his family were staring straight at Morthimas, "We accept him."

The rest of the room stood and repeated the words, some more reluctantly than others. I saw the new King relax a little as the elves accepted his rule.

"Then it is done!" The old elf raised his hands again, "King Morthimas!"

The crowd repeated the phrase with varying degrees of enthusiasm. I expected us all to be seated again, but instead the elves moved forward row by row to walk past the new King. I followed, keeping my head bowed. In with all these people, I was a bit embarrassed by my axe. It stood out loud and proud in a room conspicuous by its absence of weapons and I already stood out by virtue of my small curvy stature and black clothing. I hunched my shoulders down and moved with our row to the front.

A voice whispered in my ear, "Now, now young dwarf, you should be proud of your heritage. Stand tall."

I turned to look at the moustached face of Professor Elrond Maron. He was wearing an elven robe made of dark grey and green tweed. Fortunately this one didn't have leather patches on the elbows. I gave him a weak smile, "Good to see you."

"Do not let them make you feel ashamed, Amethyst."

I opened my mouth to make a sarcastic reply when I realised that I was feeling small and ashamed. Dzrak that! I'd been invited. I had every dzraking right to be here. I squared my shoulders and stood taller.

The Professor gave me an approving smile and nudged me forward. The elves ahead of me murmured something to their new King, half bowed and made that gesture with two fingers to their foreheads. When I arrived in front of Morthimas, I copied them as best I could.

"Well done," I murmured to him.

He smiled at me and mouthed "Thank you," before moving on to the Professor behind me. The queue continued to move and we filed outside where we were led around the clearing and then left to mill while the rest of the room got to greet their King.

"Well done!" the Professor clasped my shoulder. I smiled up at him and then was jolted to one side as Aloora greeted her favourite teacher.

"Elrond! You made it!"

"Well I wasn't going to miss the crowning of a new King. I've attended every single one in my lifetime, you know."

"How many is that?" I asked curiously.

"Well…now it's two…" the Professor's long moustache twitched.

I laughed. Elves lived so long it was unsurprising that he had only attended one other coronation. Heads turned my way. I stopped laughing. Schiztz. We were at a solemn occasion and I knew how stuffy elves could be. Lorandir appeared at my side and squeezed my hand. I felt my lips curve in a smile.

"So, it's true is it?" the Professor asked curiously, looking between us.

Lorandir nodded.

"Good for you! I thought I could sense the chemistry between you two ever since you first came to my office!"

I smiled along, wanting this line of conversation to end. Luckily, where the Professor was concerned, I could always rely on Aloora.

"Have you made any trips to the dragons while you've been here?" she interrupted and immediately monopolised the Professor's interest.

"No, not yet. Is it safe to go near them after what happened?"

"Well Agent Jones has forbidden me from going in person, but I've found a workaround. You should come with me tomorrow morning. I'm making huge strides in translating Draconic, it's fascinating really how contextual it as and…"

I drifted out of that conversation. I'd heard many such speeches about language theory before as my best friend tried to explain what her doctorate was about and her research into the ancient language of Draconic.

"Thank you for coming, I'm not sure Morty would have made the decision to go through with it if you hadn't talked to him," Lorandir met my gaze.

"Nonsense. He was always going to do the best thing for his people."

"Well thank you for being here, for me," Lorandir rubbed his thumb along my hand, sending a warm tingling feeling through my body.

"I'm not too much of a problem for you?"

The elf smiled, "There's no problem I'd rather have than you."

I hit him playfully with my free hand. He laughed. Then I frowned as I puzzled over what he had said. He had said it in a complimentary tone but the words were more insulting. Was I a problem? Was I overthinking this? More likely, but the elves around us were staring at his laugh, apparently unused to someone enjoying themselves. The unkind thought flashed through my mind before I could stop it. I began to pull away, but he kept my hand tight in his. Dzraking politics. I could feel the beginnings of a headache coming on. Before anyone could say anything, a steward moved through the crowd to Lorandir and told him that it was time for food. He nodded and led us back to the palace.

The steward cleared a path for us through the elves and it wasn't until we were back inside the room that I realised Aloora and the Professor hadn't followed us. I gazed around at the transformed space. The logs we had used for seating had been replaced with high carved wooden chairs around circular tables covered with white linen table cloths. There were about fifty tables and each could comfortably seat twenty people.

The dais remained with the throne and four other chairs now set behind a long table, facing out over the dining area. The glowing orbs of light were now sparkling against the ceiling and tall wax candles were held in simple wooden candelabras on each of the tables. Twining ivy wound around them. It looked natural and elegant…and like a fire hazard when those candles burned down to the wood. Lorandir looked around, seemingly pleased with the muted but elegant effect that had been achieved here.

"Is everyone going to eat here?"

The elf shook his head, “There are additional long tables being set up in the glade outside the palace. This space is only for the special guests.”

“Where are you sitting?” I eyed the small card with flowing Elvish written on them in front of the nearest place setting.

“Do not worry. I am sitting with you and your friend here.” He led me to one of the large round tables and walked around it until he found my name. He handed me the place card and I studied it. So that was my name in Elvish. It looked like a curling scrawl in elegant calligraphy.

“Who else is with us?” I asked as guests started to enter. They paused by a large stand at the entrance to check the seating plan.

“I’ll introduce you,” he replied breezily. I narrowed my eyes a little. That sounded too deliberately carefree. I walked around the table but couldn’t decipher the Elvish script on any of the cards. Schiztz. I was starting to get nervous about this meal.

Aloora, accompanied by the Professor, walked over to the table deep in conversation about the breeding habits of dragons. Professor Maron took his seat and looked to either side. “Delightful! I am honoured to be seated between two such gems!”

Aloora shook her head as she sat next to him. I slumped into the chair on the other side. Maybe this wouldn’t be so bad if I was between the Professor and Lorandir. I glanced around the room. The dark elves were seated in a tight group on their own table. What I thought of as the ‘regular’ elves gave their table a wide berth. I wondered what had happened to make them so wary.

Other guests started to arrive and take their seats. There was a beautiful young elf who was wearing a delicate circlet around her long blonde hair. She simpered as Lorandir introduced us and batted her eyelashes at my boyfriend. I moved my hand backwards until it was touching my axe hanging with my bag from the back of the chair. The weapon gave me the reassurance I needed to smile blandly back at the attractive elf.

The red-headed librarian joined us and Aloora tried to convince an attractive male elf to switch places so she could sit next to Shesalva. They had a heated conversation in Elvish until Lorandir pointed out that we were deliberately put male / female all around the table.

Aloora muttered something about hetero-normative standards and proceeded to talk over the male elf about the rare books in the Breconian library. It didn't sound like flirting to me, but the librarian's eyes lit up as she began to explain research she'd been doing into some newly rediscovered manuscripts from the times when stone circles were being erected. More attractive male and female elves with unpronounceable names filled our table until there were only two spots left next to Lorandir. He was looking tense and if he'd been wearing a watch, he would have been checking it.

A blonde and a brunette with tanned skin and attractive elven features glided across the room and stood at the spots. They seemed familiar but I couldn't place where I knew them from, after all, it wasn't like I routinely hung out with elves. I mean if you didn't count Lorandir. I looked at my other half and noticed the slightly straighter back and the forced smile. He stepped forward and held first the lady then the man by the elbows leaning forward to press foreheads together. He hadn't greeted any of the other guests at our table this way. I had a bad feeling about this.

He swallowed tightly and turned to me, "Amethyst, I'm pleased to introduce you to my parents, Zaladasha and Bovolmiras."

Chapter 7

Schiztz, schiztz, schiztz! His parents! I was unprepared. I wiped my suddenly sweaty palms on my flimsy skirt and stood slowly. I took a breath and stepped towards them, careful to keep my face blank. They looked like they were in their early forties, but then Lorandir looked younger than me and he was over a hundred years old!

"It's an honour to meet you," I managed. I held out my hand. His mother looked at it for a moment and blinked, then she took my fingers lightly. She held my hand for the briefest moment then released me. His father followed suit, giving me a more traditional handshake. I wouldn't say it was friendly but it was slightly warmer than the frosty touch his mother had given me. Maybe fridge temperature rather than arctic.

"The honour is ours. I'm not sure we've met a dwarf before."

I was proud that I didn't wince, instead I glanced at Lorandir, "Er, Lorandir didn't mention you'd be joining us…" We would be having words about that later.

"Of course we would not have missed my brother's funeral, even if we were half way around the world," his mother replied, her green eyes sparkling with unshed tears. It was then that I realised why I had recognised them. Lorandir's eyes were the exact colour and shape as his mother's while his nose was the mirror image of his father's; it was the family resemblance I had spotted.

"Yeah, of course…"

"I believe you know Jilania?" his mother talked across me and indicated the simpering blonde elf across the table. She flashed a megawatt smile and I could almost feel the young elf's glamour project across the table. She stood and sashayed around the table until she was standing between Lorandir and his parents.

"Hello," she breathed in an impersonation of Marilyn Monroe that was almost laughable. I wondered if glamour worked on other elves. If it did, Lorandir was a goner. There was no way I could compete with a stick thin model. I was immune to the glamour, thanks to a charm Gunther had given me, but even without it she was attractive with sleek hair and chiselled cheekbones.

"Of course," Lorandir replied smoothly reaching for my hand, "I remember you used to chase Morthimas around like a sad puppy while we were still schooling here. Shall we sit?"

I sat down while she swayed back to her seat, her robe somehow managing to accentuate the sexiness of her walk. If we had been in a roomful of humans, every eye would have been on her. Here, only about fifty per cent of males turned to watch her performance.

Everyone else around the table was watching our exchange with interest. I stared at my plate, made of wood of course, and felt my cheeks flushing scarlet. I moved my knives and forks as if I was rearranging them into alignment. Lorandir reached up and squeezed my hand comfortingly. I forced myself to breathe.

Professor Maron broke the silence, "Prince Bovolmiras, how are the German forests these days? I understand you've been there for the past few years."

"You are incredibly well informed Elrond, well actually our German cousins are having similar difficulties containing magical creatures. Their realm is close to fae as well, so their defensive techniques are quite intricate."

I let the conversation wash over me. I thought about pretending I was sick so I wouldn't have to deal with all this, whatever exactly this was. Just as I'd made the decision to get up and go back to Lorandir's room, Morthimas strode onto the dais wearing his new crown.

He stood for a moment in front of the table and waited for everyone to quiet down. Most of the elves were looking at him with polite patience, although some had open scepticism on their faces like they were waiting for him to slip up. Mordred was gazing at him with an expression I couldn't fathom – it might have been jealousy. I tried to keep my face neutral and my hands still as I watched him raise his arms.

"Welcome friends, both old and new," he inclined his head towards our table at the word 'new'. I pushed myself back in my chair. "It is with sadness and humility that I have accepted this crown. Sadness at my father's death and humility in knowing that a greater man than I made such a grave mistake."

Mutterings carried across the room. I thought I knew what they were thinking. A dzraking big mistake to steal a dragon egg.

"It has occurred to me that a King must be surrounded not only by those he trusts but also those who can bring different points of view. As a new ruler, I will be guided by the Elven High Council," murmurs of approval sounded from the tables. "To ensure the Council can help me be a wise and just ruler, it must be formed of the best candidates," more sounds of approval, but I noticed strained smiles on the faces of the three elves sitting behind the table on the stage.

It might have been my imagination, but I was almost certain the one I'd encountered earlier glanced at Mordred. The dark elf didn't return his gaze but instead speared Morthimas with an intense look as the King continued his speech.

"I wish to thank the councillors for their service," he turned and nodded towards the three elves behind him. They raised their glasses and inclined their heads. Their smiles still looked tense.

"We are in modern times and cannot ignore the world moving beyond our borders. To help me navigate these new times will require new ways of thinking, we must learn to integrate more with the mundane world and its technologies. So, I will undertake a period of selection to decide on the most appropriate members of the Council going forward. I encourage anyone, of any age, to apply. My cousin will post the details tomorrow. Now, please, enjoy your meals."

The elves sat in shocked silence as their new King sat at the table and confidently helped himself to a glass of water.

"You can't do that!" erupted an elf with brown hair from near the back of the room.

Two guards starting edging towards the elf. Morthimas waved them off and then stared coolly at the standing elf, looking every bit the detached ruler. "It is done. And I assure you that the best candidates will be selected in a fair process. I want to avoid the mistakes my father made and need the very best advisors to be able to do that."

The dissenter sat back down and muttered to the rest of his table. I noticed that while some elves were shocked and disapproving, some were chattering excitedly. I guessed this was unusual kingly behaviour.

"Good for Morthimas." Everyone turned to stare at me. Schiztz. I had said my thoughts out loud.

"How dare she comment on our traditions?" Lorandir's mother hissed in Elvish to her son. Too bad I could understand her.

"Mother…"

"Really! What does she know about anything?"

I couldn't keep my mouth shut, "I know Morthimas will be a better ruler if he feels he can trust his Council. Those elves didn't know his father well enough to stop him making a stupid decision, or worse, they knew about it and still didn't stop him. I don't blame Morthimas for wanting to have people he can trust around him."

Lorandir's mother blinked at me, "I see," she said pointedly, "My son did not mention that you could understand Elvish. It seems there is a lot he hasn't told me."

I shifted uncomfortably in my seat. Maybe I should just get up and go. I started to rise, but efficient waiters swooped in with large wooden trays laden with food on small plates. Starters were served. One of them was placed in front of me and I gazed at the three meagre mouthfuls of elven fare on the tiny plate. My evening was going from bad to worse.

I picked delicately at the food, recognising the pink looking confection as the disgusting fish-tasting entrée I'd tried at the ball. At least I wasn't going to look like a pig. I pushed it around my plate with a fork, making it look like I'd eaten something and instead took a long drink of the cool white wine the waiters had filled our glasses with. The alcohol went straight to my head and a pleasant wooziness took the edge off the evening. I kept quiet as the table debated who the best candidates were for the Council and the behaviour of the dragons.

As dessert came, I could almost enjoy the creamy chocolate mousse, so light it almost evaporated as it entered my mouth. If only all elven food could be like this. The elves had provided spoons with the longest handles and tiniest shallow bowl shape on the end of it. It took me an age to finish the pudding and I savoured every bite. I was using the spoon to scrape the sides of the delicate dish that had contained the mousse when a shadow crossed over the table. I looked up to see Mordred walking behind my chair. I stiffened involuntarily and my hand moved subconsciously to the jewel around my neck. The dark elf ignored me though and instead bent his head to speak to Aloora.

"I had not realised we were in the presence of one of the foremost dragon experts in the world," he took her hand and brought it to his lips, "I am honoured to make your acquaintance Ms Dragonquest."

The table had gone silent, watching the dark elf with nervous expressions. Aloora looked somewhat bemused by the greeting, and I was expecting her to make a comment about how inappropriate it was for him to kiss her hand, but she must have had a lot of wine because instead she smiled and replied in elvish, "And a pleasure to meet you…"

The dark elf bowed lower, "Please, call me Mordred. I would very much enjoy speaking to you about dragons during our stay here."

Aloora was clearly torn between her pet topic and wanting to spend time with Shesalva. I didn't think I was imagining the glimmer of attraction that was simmering between those two.

"Perhaps tomorrow…" the gnome replied.

"Of course, until then." Mordred clicked his heels together and bowed before turning to leave. The other elves resumed their conversations, throwing anxious glances over their shoulders as the dark elf walked away, his black ensemble standing out among the more natural colours that the elves favoured.

Professor Elrond shifted in his seat and pursed his lips but said nothing.

After more small talk and pointed silences from Lorandir's mother, we returned to our rooms. It was all very formal and almost the opposite of a dwarven or even a mundane human wake where there would have been some celebration of the person's life. Not what I would choose for my funeral for sure.

I was safely back in Lorandir's room, snuggled up in the warm linen bedclothes while he made tea in the kitchen area, when I heard the knock on the closed wooden door.

Chapter 8

I wrapped the sheets around myself and padded to the top of the staircase, my necklace hanging low over the superhero t-shirt I used as pyjamas. Voices carried up to me and I stopped before I was in sight. His parents were here.

"Really, a dwarf?!"

"I am not having this conversation with you!"

"But…a dwarf!"

"Don't you want me to be happy?"

"Of course, but you should not delude yourself, son. I suppose if you want to have some fun then that is alright, but really, do you see this lasting?"

"Yes!" I heard the exasperation mounting in Lorandir's voice.

"And what about when she dies? Have you thought about that?"

"Yes," his voice was more sombre this time, "of course I have…but I would rather have a few short years with her than a lifetime without her."

"And her dwarven blood means she will live longer than a human…"

"You are no help at all Bovolmiras! Well when this ends, as it will, we will of course be here for you, son." His mother was quiet then, which I guessed meant she had gone.

"You've done alright there, son, and your mother, well, she will come around." So his Dad liked me a bit then. That was something I suppose. I tiptoed back into the bedroom and lay on the bed facing away from the door. Dark thoughts began to surface.

We hadn't even really begun our relationship and it was already causing rifts in his family. He hadn't even met my parents yet. My mind raced with all the horrible possibilities from that encounter. I didn't hear my lover come in but I felt the pressure on the bed as he climbed in next to me. I closed my eyes and breathed steadily. It was a coward's way out but I didn't feel like talking about this evening.

I heard his soft sigh and felt the light brush of his lips on my hair before he settled down. His breath soon fell into the steady rhythm of deep sleep. I stayed awake staring at the wall in the dark room, wondering about the future and what we had both gotten ourselves into.

Eventually, I couldn't take it anymore. I eased myself out of the comfortable bed and threw on some jeans and my cardigan.

"What are you doing?"

Dzraking elven hearing. I should have known I wouldn't have been able to sneak out without waking Lorandir.

"I can't sleep."

Silence.

"I'm going for a quick walk to clear my head."

A loud sigh, “Let me come with you.”

“No really, it’s fine. I’ll just do a quick lap around the palace then come back here.”

“I don’t like the thought of you walking alone at night.”

I snorted, “This palace is full of guards. Seriously, what could happen?”

I sensed the elf’s frown in the darkness.

“If it makes you feel any better, I can take my axe…”

“Alright, but if you’re not back in fifteen minutes, I’m coming to find you.”

“Yes sir!” I let off a mock salute and picked up my axe and my phone. It wasn’t fair of me to take my bad mood out on my lover, but I needed to think. And this whole place was too dzraking elven.

I muttered the magic word that unlocked the door and headed out of Lorandir’s quarters. Almost as soon as I left the room, I knew that I’d made a mistake. I turned back to see the door sealing itself shut, the joins disappearing back into Lorandir’s family crest. Dzrak.

Grumbling to myself, I considered walking through the portal that was casting a faint glow across the corridor, but decided against it. My stomach was churning thanks to the exotic elven fare I’d consumed – I wasn’t even sure now that the pudding had been chocolate, surely chocolate would never turn on me like this – and the thought of the travel sickness I experienced from portal travel was enough to make me pad along the corridor instead.

I had no real thought of where I was going except that I wanted to walk. And think. I balanced Bane on one shoulder as I walked, enjoying the solid comforting weight of my ancestral weapon. It helped me forget that I was high up in the tree, far from solid ground.

The corridor branched off into several hallways. I picked one at random and followed it, wondering how exactly the elves had created this palace. I was tracing the whorls of a knot in the wood when I felt the air change.

I looked up. And nearly threw up. There, in front of me, was an open doorway that led to nothing. The cool night air lifted my hair as a soft breeze blew past. That was the change in air. I was at one of the many exits from the palace. Logically I knew that there would be a staircase and it wasn't a sheer drop but that didn't stop my palms from sweating or my knees from buckling. The elves didn't deign to design handrails. The sure-footed people didn't need anything to lean on as they traversed the high walkways of the forest. But I wasn't an elf.

I forced myself to take several deep breaths while I kept one hand connected to the wooden wall. My eyes focused on the dark opening in a perverse fascination. I couldn't look away. I couldn't stop imagining what it would feel like to take a step out of the door and fall. How long would it take to reach the ground? I shuddered and pressed my hand more forcefully against the wall. When my legs could work again, I took three large steps backwards, away from the drop.

That short distance broke the spell of my own fear and I could walk again. I turned and went back the way I'd come. At the place where the corridor had opened up, I stalled. I couldn't remember which path led back to the safety of Lorandir's room.

"Lorandir," I whispered, hoping against hope that his keen elven ears would hear me. Nothing. I tried again. This time I thought I did hear something. I headed down one of the corridors, glad of the strange glowing bugs that moved slowly along the ceiling. The voices got louder. I hurried forward, glad to be in company after my fright.

As I moved closer, their words became clearer.

"…the elven forces are depleted after years of peace. The treaties with the mundane world have made them weak."

"All must be ready by the Winter Solstice."

"But my lord, the new King has disbanded the council, I may not be able to advise him…"

"I commend you for your concern, but it is the King's right to have who he wishes on the council. I trust you will help him with a diligent search for the right council members."

"But…"

"A diligent, long search."

I frowned. It sounded like they were talking about Morthimas. Suddenly I wanted to be far away from whoever these people were. I turned and Bane thudded into the wall.

"What was that?"

"Someone's there!"

Dzrak! I weighed my options. Stay or run. I turned, ready to flee, knowing I was no match for elven speed. And collided with Lorandir's bare torso. We went sprawling onto the floor.

"What the -?" he didn't get any further.

Mordred and the councillor with the long white hair appeared behind me, their hands aglow with magic. They appraised the scene. I clambered to my feet and gripped my axe. Lorandir righted himself and looked between my fighting stance and the flustered elder elves.

Mordred laughed, his dark eyes glowing sinisterly in the greenish light from the glow bugs, “Prince Lorandir and his dwarf lady. You gave us quite a fright.”

“What were you doing meeting up in the middle of the night?”

“My, my, what an imagination you have. We were remembering the late King and discussing the future. What, pray tell were you doing creeping around the palace?”

“I got lost,” I didn’t like how defensive my voice sounded.

“Then how fortunate that your prince was here to save you,” Mordred bowed tightly, turned on his heels and walked back the way he’d come. The councillor headed back in a different direction, frowning over his shoulder as he went.

“What was all that about?” asked Lorandir.

Chapter 9

Morning came and soft sunlight shone through the large window in Lorandir's room. It was open. I stretched and found his side of the bed empty. I had told him about the strange snippet of conversation I'd heard We had stayed up too late talking it over but he hadn't been able to understand it any more than I had.

I stifled a yawn, blinked myself awake and pulled on a silky dressing gown hanging on the back of the bathroom door. On an elf, it would come to their knees, on me it was almost floor length. I walked slowly to the large open window, more like a door; it led to a balcony formed of sculpted branches. I heard a twanging noise followed by a thud.

I forced myself to look up at the canopy and not consider how high we were. At least it wasn't a sheer drop, I shuddered, like last night. I inched my way forward to the edge of the balcony, crossing my arms and clenching my upper arms as if that would stop my head from reeling. There was a balustrade formed of twining ivy. It looked more decorative than a barrier that would prevent me plummeting to my death from an elven palace. I tried to ignore that thought.

I reached the ivy and uncrossed my arms. My nails had dug small crescent marks into my skin through the flimsy dressing gown. I gripped the handrail tightly, my knuckles white against the green leaves. The faint twang sounded again.

I turned my head to the source of the noise and there, high up in the canopy, balancing on a slender branch was Lorandir. He had a bow in his arms and was aiming at a target I couldn't see. A stiff breeze caused the leaves to rustle and the branch swayed.

I let out an involuntary cry, worried he would fall as he adjusted his balance. He turned at my cry and gave me a smile before rushing daintily down the branches. Each time he crossed to a new branch, my stomach turned and I felt sick. He was by my side in a few seconds. His smile turned to concern.

"You look pale."

"Heights."

He smiled again and took my hands from the railing. I felt the small callouses forming on his fingers where he had used the bow. They were reassuring against my own rough hands, toughened from handling the tools of my jewellery trade and a few burns from the heat of Errol's flames. I didn't protest as he led me away from the edge. Back inside his room, I started shaking.

"Were you worried for me galad'Amethysta?"

"You could have killed yourself!"

He laughed at that and kissed my forehead. “I practiced up there every day growing up and never fell, even in force nine gales,” he shrugged, “a morning breeze wasn’t going to kill me.”

I sank onto the bed. Elves were dextrous and agile and had great balance. I would never get used to heights.

“I’ll make you a cup of coffee.”

I perked up at that. A strong cup of coffee was just what I needed, but I hadn’t seen any when I was searching in the kitchen area yesterday. I was about to say something when Lorandir bent and rummaged in his bag. He dug out a packet of rich instant coffee, much better than the supermarket own brand stuff I bought myself back at home. My heart swelled. He really knew me.

He sauntered downstairs and I heard the sound of wooden mugs hitting counters as he made the hot drinks. The elf brought them upstairs and we sat on the bed drinking. After a couple of sips, I was ready to talk.

“So, your parents…” He continued to sip his own tea, eyeing me carefully. I carried on “... they don't seem to like me very much …”

“Does that matter?”

“Does it matter to you?”

“All that matters to me is that I'm with you.”

A fuzzy warm feeling grew in my stomach. I pushed it down, “But aren't you worried about the future?”

This was the first time we had spoken about a future together. Both of us had been living in the moment and enjoying our time together. I took a drink to cover my nervousness. I might just have blown our relationship.

He met my eyes with an intensity I recognised, “This year has been the craziest in over a century for me, and all I know is I want to be with you.”

That warm fuzzy feeling came back. Maybe it didn't matter if his parents didn't like me. When he looked at me with those bright green eyes I felt like anything was possible. I put my mug down on the small bedside table and moved towards him. Somehow he was no longer holding his own cup and his arms were around me as we embraced. My world narrowed and when I felt the familiar heat of his magic touch my skin, I found I could ignore everything except his hands and mouth.

Later, after we were both satisfied, I closed my eyes, “I could spend all day here with you.”

Lorandir stroked my cheek and a half smile played over his lips, “We have to get dressed, I have a surprise for you.”

My eyes opened and then narrowed. He had a playful look about him and I wasn't sure what that meant, “What is it?”

“Oh no, I'm not spoiling the surprise. You'll see when we get there.”

It was with some trepidation that I got dressed and followed him through the portal which seemed to have been set up permanently between his room and the ground. The last time he had taken me somewhere for a surprise in this elven city, we had ended up being attacked by a chimera. Not a pleasant experience.

This time though he led me into the city itself. We crossed over the beautiful bridges created from tree roots and into to what seems to me to be a thoroughfare. A few tall elves were walking along carrying hessian bags, chatting and generally going about their lives. Was this a shopping street? I couldn't see anything at ground level so I turned my gaze upwards towards the treetops; there I saw more activity as elves crossed swinging bridges that spanned the gaps between the trees. None of the walkways had any sort of handrail. It made me queasy just thinking about crossing those structures. I hoped we weren't going up there. Lorandir tucked my hand into the crook of his arm and we moved along at a slow pace. Just as I was about to ask again where we were going, he turned off down what seem to be a side street.

I heard a familiar clanging and my ears perked up. It sounded like the regular hammer beats of metal upon metal. My step quickened involuntarily and Lorandir smiled as we moved towards the source of the noise. We stopped in front of a large tree stump. Tree stump hardly did it justice. It was enormous. There was no door so I could see in to where a burly elf was taking a glowing piece of metal from a forge with long tongs. He struck it with a large hammer against an anvil. Behind the anvil, coals glowed hot red against metallic black in a neat forge. I marvelled that the stump hadn't burnt down.

The smith caught sight of us and turned. His face was openly curious as he took me in. Lorandir smiled at him, "Hello there Foral, this is Amethyst."

"Amethyst, a pleasure to meet you," his smile seemed genuine and he stepped towards me with his hand out. I noticed a limp and the thud of metal on wood as he walked. I smiled back and shook his hand, keeping my eyes averted from his metallic leg.

“And you Foral, I've never met an elven smith before.”

“Foral made the charm you were interested in. The one that linked me and… Espretha.”

I ignored the pang of guilt that washed through me at the knowledge that I was training with his former friend and instead looked at the smith with renewed interest, this elf had made a pair of charms that locked onto different magical signatures meaning that the owners could locate each other and communicate feelings almost telepathically. It was his charms that had given me the idea for unlosable jewellery. I was very interested.

“Lorandir tells me that you designed the first piece of true dragon jewellery we’ve seen in millennia. You have to tell me more. And is that a dwarven axe? I’ve never seen one in person before!” I was taken aback by his positivity as he limped towards me. He held his hands over the blade with reverence.

“May I?”

I slipped Bane from its holster and handed it to the smith. He held it in awe, then took a couple of test swings.

“Perfectly balanced, naturally…and can I sense elven magic?”

“Lorandir enchanted it so it’s invisible unless I’m close to someone. It helps for carrying it on the streets. I wasn’t sure the axe would take the enchantment but it seems to work…”

I took the axe back and walked out of the forge. When I was about six feet away, Foral’s eyes widened as the axe faded from sight. I smiled and stepped forward again. Foral took the weapon again and admired it anew. He asked me about the markings and I began to point out the Dwarfish runes etched into the axe head and what they meant. Foral listened eagerly and asked questions about some of the runes that looked similar but had different meanings.

"I've got to go and help Morthimas, will you be alright here?"

I nodded vaguely at Lorandir. I was already lost in the joy of talking to another crafter about their work. He kissed me on the head and left.

With a final swing of my axe, Foral handed it back, "Thank you for that, I thought I would live forever without handling a dwarf-forged axe. And the axe of Amethyst Haernson, fighter of dragons to boot! Truly, this is something I shall tell my children."

I shifted uncomfortably and decided to change the subject, "So, you can create metal that links magical signatures?"

"Yes, it's tricky but doable. Why don't I show you?"

We spent the morning together with him trying to teach me how to meld the magic into the metal. Elven magic was all about nature and working with the materials, settling the magic on the piece. Foral used some of the leaves that fell from the forest trees to help him focus his magic. The leaves burned away in the heat as we worked the metal but it left his magic imprinted on the charm he created.

It was totally different to the dwarven way of working which involved shaping metal to our will and using runes. I couldn't quite get the hang of letting the power settle into the charms we were working with rather than enchanting it to do something and leaves were of no help to my magic. I made some progress though. By lunchtime, I had managed to layer my power onto a key ring. It was a strange feeling unlike any of my usual jewellery; I could sense it like a soft niggle in the back of my mind.

"The next step when you practice at home is to add another's magic to the same piece and then once you have done that, remove your own magic."

"How do I do that?"

"Well…"

"Amethyst! We need to go now!"

I turned to see Aloora panting heavily in the entrance to the forge. Lorandir was standing behind her glancing round nervously. He kept looking up, as if something was going to swoop down from the sky. I noticed he was carrying a bow with an arrow nocked against the string. I grabbed my axe and flattened myself against the wall, also looking up. Foral had conjured up a mace from somewhere and was following our gazes.

"What's happened?" I hissed.

"You know I was going to try to get some more recordings from the dragons…"

I closed my eyes. I knew my friend's obsession was going to get us all killed, "What did you do?"

"Well Mordred was really excited about it too and we were discussing Draconic imperative tenses. It was going great except Agent Jones said I couldn't get too close to them anymore so I decided to use a drone." I groaned as Aloora carried on, “Anyway, I coated the drone with the unguent,” I grimaced at the memory of the stinky paste she had forced me to use last time we were in Breconia. Aloora rolled her eyes at me and continued, “So it was undetectable but…well the dragons noticed it and...”

“Let me guess: dragons – one, drone – nil?”

“Pretty much, and they’re so territorial, it’s fascinating really, but anyway they are quite distressed and so the elves are getting distressed and Mordred’s already gone and I think it’s best we leave. Now. Right now. We’re taking the Professor back with us too, so let’s go.”

“But all my things are back at the palace!”

“Meet at the van in fifteen minutes,” Aloora raced off.

“Schiztz!” I swore, “I guess I’d better go back. Sorry Foral, it was lovely to meet you, maybe we can do it again some time and if you’re ever in Cardiff, look me up.”

The smith nodded distractedly, still keeping his gaze on the sky through his tree stump forge. I pocketed my key chain and jogged back to the palace. I thought I heard a roar sound from somewhere out to the left of the elven city. I sped up. Lorandir matched my pace easily. I remembered my training with Espretha, the elven traitor, and focused on my breathing rather than dragons that may or may not be about to destroy Breconia. I was still running as we headed through the portal that took us back to Lorandir’s room. Once inside, I scrambled upstairs and stuffed everything I’d brought into my backpack. The elf was packing too. I looked at him questioningly.

He shrugged, "Things are a little delicate now, especially with the dragons being…agitated, so Morty agrees that it's best I head back to Cardiff for a while."

That was that then. All packed, we dashed back through the portal. Someone had changed its settings since we had entered the palace and this time we staggered out into the car park on the outskirts of the reserve. I lurched to one side as I waited for the ground to stop spinning and the rainbows to disappear from my vision. I heard an engine rev loudly. Aloora was already in the van. I heard the roar again and looked up. Schiztz.

A red dragon the size of a bus was swooping around the mountains that loomed to one side of the forest city. Distressed was an understatement. It looked thoroughly pissed. I raced to the van and threw my bag into the back. I strapped myself into one of the seats and gripped Bane tightly as I shrank into the multi-coloured woollen blankets that covered the chairs. Lorandir swung himself in behind me and shut the door. Professor Maron was already in the front seat next to Aloora. His eyes were shining at the excitement of being so close to his beloved dragons.

Aloora put her foot down and the van reversed hard. I cringed as we stopped millimetres from the bright purple Rolls Royce. Aloora shifted gears and with a squeal of protest, the van set off, leaving a dust cloud in its wake. I checked the window.

"It's following us!"

As if spurred on by movement, the dragon had changed course above the mountain and was heading for us. Aloora twisted in her seat to try to see it.

"Focus on the road!"

She grunted and shoved her phone into the Professor's hands as she accelerated hard. "Come on Dan…" she cajoled the van as it sped up. The dragon was nearly on us. I could not believe the Professor was filming the creature that was trying to kill us.

I heard its deafening roar and wished I had used the toilet before we fled from the palace. I gripped my axe and activated its shield, in case that would do any good. I heard Lorandir mutter the Dwarfish word "Sheld," as he activated the shield I had enchanted into his sword when we had first met. The Professor was gripping the sides of his seat so hard his knuckles had gone white.

A shadow crossed the van as the dragon flew over us. Something hit the roof of the van hard. I watched as a white metal object spun off onto the road behind us. It looked like it had been mauled by the dragon, which I guessed it had been.

"Poor Simone…" Aloora sighed.

"Simone?"

"Simone the drone…what am I going to tell Dot? She loved that thing."

I gaped at my friend worrying about the drone at a time like this. The dragon had veered off to one side and now changed course again heading for the van. As it approached the magical barrier that protected the reserve from the rest of the world, it did a loop and was now facing us. I saw its mouth open and its throat glowed red before it sent a stream of fire towards the van. Aloora grimaced and kept going into the flames. I prayed the combined shields would protect us from the heat of the blaze.

Aloora twisted in her seat, "Activate the rune!"

"What?" I stared at her dumbly.

"The fire rune! Now!"

I unbuckled my seatbelt and sank to the floor of the van where I had etched a fire rune when we were under attacked from ten-legged spider monsters on the way to Stonehenge. I spoke the activation word and poured my power into it, creating an inferno that built on the dragon's flames. It was difficult to see through the fire. Aloora pressed the brakes and we skidded to a halt. She cut the engine. The dragon roared. Wings swept through the air, close enough that the van rocked in the force of the down draft. It was circling us.

Chapter 10

Silence loomed over the van. We waited. Each of us scanned the windows, searching for signs of approaching death.

"OK, that should be enough. Let the flames die down slowly."

I did as Aloora asked, keeping my head turned towards the window, waiting for the dragon to swoop in and kill us all. Nothing. We stayed quiet.

"I think it's gone."

No one moved.

"Perhaps we should all just wait a few more minutes, just to be sure," the Professor spoke what was in all our heads. We waited nervously for five minutes then Aloora started the van. She drove cautiously through the magical barrier and then we were out on the main road.

"Good thing Agent Jones had the engine warded to protect it from flames or that wouldn't have worked!" Aloora broke the silence.

"Do you mind stopping the van at your earliest convenience young Dragonquest, I think I need to…" The

Professor had turned a shade of pale green. Aloora pulled the van over to the verge and stopped hard. The elderly elf staggered out and was violently sick over the grass. We exchanged worried glances but after a couple of minutes, he sank back into his seat and strapped himself in.

"Great idea of yours Dragonquest, and to think we must be the only people alive to have witnessed a dragon's blaze and survived. Quite remarkable!" Now he had voided his stomach and we were heading further away from the dragons, the Professor seemed to be returning to his optimistic self.

Lorandir reached across and squeezed my hand. We had both experienced the horror of seeing the red dragon awaken and destroy part of Cardiff Castle. Neither of us were as enthusiastic about dragons as Aloora and Professor Maron.

The rest of the road trip passed uneventfully. Aloora and the Professor debated whether they could put this experience in an academic paper entitled *Dragon Response to Drones: Fight or Flight*. Lorandir and I played a half-hearted game of eye spy so we didn't have to engage with that discussion.

After using the facilities at a run-down service station and grabbing some tired looking sandwiches for lunch, I managed to snooze through Aloora's erratic driving until we got back to our flat. Aloora had already dropped the Professor back at Cardiff University's main building, where he seemed to live as well as work.

She parked the van next to Marco's old Volkswagen, got out her phone and started to upload the video of the dragon chasing us to her social media channels. I shook my head behind her back. Her internet presence was a constant feature in our friendship. One I didn't always appreciate. It was late afternoon, the sun hung low in the sky. I turned to ask Lorandir what he was up to for the rest of the day.

"I should probably call Morty and find out how the rest of his interviews for Council positions went…and I should call my parents too. I left without a chance to say goodbye. I'll call you later?"

I nodded. I didn't want to be present for either call and I needed a shower. I kissed the elf goodbye, feeling myself start to blush as I always did with any public display of affection. It didn't help that a group of local kids were snickering as they took a break from kicking a ball against the wall. I ignored them, grabbed my things out of the van and trooped upstairs to our large flat as Lorandir loped off to his own place.

As soon as I walked in the door, Errol jumped up, pleased to see me. He alternated between trying to lick me with his pointed tongue and blowing small excited flames from his nostrils. I smiled and tickled him behind his ears.

"Did you miss me boy? Were you a good boy for Marco?"

"'E was fine. A bit enthusiastic about 'elping me with the table but fine," Marco lifted up his fingers to show me a couple of bright burn marks. I winced. I knew too well what that felt like – it was an occupational hazard of using Errol to help with my trade. I knew what would help too. I dumped my bag and my axe next to the distressed table that now dominated our shared living space and went to my room.

"Try this," I tossed a mostly empty tube of salve at Marco. He caught it with one hand and read the tube out loud.

"Madam Mim's burn ointment?"

"It really works, just rub a bit on the burn and it'll feel better in no time."

He shrugged and opened the tube. His nose wrinkled at the sulphuric scent that wafted from the medicine but he rubbed a small amount of the bright yellow ointment onto his skin. After a couple of seconds he stopped swearing and looked at me, "OK, that does feel better."

"By the time you go to bed, it'll be completely healed. Why don't you keep the tube, I need to get a new one anyway."

"Thank you, do you want to watch the TV? It's a new series of *Best Homes Budget Makeover – Extreme Edition*."

I shook my head and instead checked the fridge. A brightly coloured flyer fell off as I opened it. I groaned aloud at the contents. Healthy salads, oat milk and eggs. No comfort food. I needed to shop. I shut the fridge and picked up the flyer. It was for a supernatural drag show at the vampire bar *Blud* - no points for originality with that name - with a selection of warm up nights at a couple of other magic friendly places in the city. I noted the Goat was one of the locations and wondered how they could fit a stage in the olde worlde pub. I used a magnet to reattach it to the fridge door and moved my things to my bedroom. I was slightly dismayed that Errol chose to curl up next to Marco on the sofa. He almost seemed to be watching the TV programme. No accounting for taste. I unpacked and put about half of my clothes in the wash basket before I slumped on the bed and fell asleep.

The next few days passed in much the same way. Lorandir was busy doing whatever it was he did that constituted a job. From the snippets I could pick up from our text chats he was helping his cousin not to freak out and choose a new Council. True to the strange conversation I'd overheard, the white-haired Councilmember was drawing out the process by recommending dozens of potential candidates and then insisting on vetting them all thoroughly before allowing the King to interview anyone.

Marco watched repeats of makeover shows and using Errol to help char some wood into a distressed effect. Aloora was either working or studying. I was bored and had no plans.

I thought about my options for the evening: I could watch a superhero film on my laptop or read one of my fantasy novels. I could call my parents. I swiftly ruled out that option; they were likely to be in their new hot tub making the most of the late winter sunshine and I didn't need that image in my head. What I really wanted was to burn off some of the energy I seemed to have so I could think clearly about everything that had happened in Breconia. I had met Lorandir's parents, discovered more about how to make the charms that I was sure could lead to unlosable jewellery, and I'd escaped a dragon attack. Again. There was only one person who could help me clear my head. I got out my smartphone and called Espretha.

"Hey, you up for some training?"

"Always. It's getting dark – meet at the usual place?"

"Sure, be there soon."

That was one thing I liked about the elf, she was always straight to the point. We had spent so much time training together, I was starting to consider her a friend…even if she had been part of a cult that had awakened the first dzraking dragon and started all these complications in my life.

I changed into the comfortable jogging bottoms, body armour vest and oversized t-shirt that comprised my workout gear, strung my axe diagonally over my back in a custom-made harness and pulled on my cycling helmet. As I was wresting my bike down from the rack we had put in the entrance hall, Aloora came back out of her room. She narrowed her eyes at me.

"Where are you going?"

"Training. I'll be back later."

"I'll give you a lift. I've got to take the van back to the Office and might as well do it now."

"Cheers," that would save me wearing myself out before I'd gone one round with the elf. She was fast enough without me giving her any advantage.

Aloora picked up the van's keys from the ceramic bowl we kept on a tall wooden table near the door. As well as keys, it also had an open packet of chewing gum, a couple of pennies and spare Allen keys and components that we had left over after putting together the pieces of streamlined Swedish flat pack furniture Aloora had insisted we needed for the flat. I was always a little nervous using the chairs when we had eight screws that apparently didn't go anywhere. Ally said they were spares but I wasn't so sure.

"See you later Marco," I called.

“See you later, and if that table isn’t moved out of our lounge by the end of the week, I’m going to remodel your bedroom so it’s all modern minimalist!” Aloora threatened.

Marco gave us a lazy wave from the sofa and ignored Aloora’s jibe about the table and his bedroom. Their tastes were so different, it left us with an apartment that was part sleek modern furniture, part shabby chic upcycled pieces and totally mismatched. It didn’t help that Aloora’s books and scrolls constantly spread out of her room and into our shared living space. She swore she didn’t do it on purpose, but unless they were sentient and had decided to strike off for a better life with more space in our living room rather than stay on her bookshelves, I couldn’t see how else they got there.

We drove to the city centre with Aloora’s preferred epic fantasy music blaring from the van’s speakers. She pulled up outside the entrance to Bute Park with complete disregard for the double yellow lines and no parking signs. I hopped out.

“How are you getting back to the flat?”

Aloora just shrugged and gestured for me to close the door before a police car showed up. I frowned as I shut the door and stepped onto the pavement. I felt like something was going on but had no idea what it was.

Still scowling, I shouldered my axe and headed to the park. I avoided looking at the creepy stone statues that lined the wall. Their glass eyes and lifelike carving made the animals look like they could come to life at any moment. I hurried in to find Espretha.

She was lounging against a large tree in our usual practice spot, looking elegant and deadly as she picked her teeth with the point of a sharp dagger.

"I thought you were away at the funeral?"

"I was."

"How was it?"

"Elven with a touch of dragon thrown in for flair."

The elf snorted as she tried not to laugh, "No wonder you're back early. Let's get started. Defend!"

She launched herself at me as I struggled to wrest Bane from its harness. I sidestepped while I tugged at the handle. She pivoted and came at me again. This time I gave up on trying to wrench the axe free and instead slipped the shoulder strap off and grabbed the axe as it fell from my back.

I whirled it up towards her face, forcing her to step back. She changed tact and feinted left. I was ready and moved in. Over the course of our sessions, I had learned that she had the advantage when she could use her speed and agility to surprise me, but if I got in close and grappled her, my weight meant I had a fair chance of pinning her…as long as she didn't use any of her martial arts tricks to get out of my hold. As she twisted, I met her blades with my axe handle and turned so one of my double-headed axe's blades was aimed at her stomach. I swung the axe hard. She grunted and leapt backwards.

"You're getting better!"

Then she ran at me. I swung again, more wildly this time, over extending my reach. Schiztz. The elf jumped and used my shoulder as a push off point to get behind me. In less than a second she had one of her knives at my throat and the other twisting into my side. Cheat.

"Still need practice though," she laughed as she released me.

I groaned and rubbed my neck.

"Again!"

We had three more bouts as the sun set that all ended with me getting a knife too close to my skin for comfort before I called it a day. Even my superior night vision hadn't given me much of an advantage thanks to the electric streetlights that filled the sky with their orange and white glow. I had only managed to get close to her once and, although she had got her knife to my neck, I had managed to pull my own from my ankle holster and pressed it to her stomach. The elf had grinned at the stalemate before suggesting a run to cool down. I begged to be let off.

"OK," she surprised me by agreeing so easily to letting me out of a run, "what are you doing tonight?"

"Nothing…" I wondered where this was going.

"How about a drink?"

"Sure," I considered our weapons and attire. There was only really one place to suggest, "The Goat?"

As we approached, the pub sign swayed in the breeze lending the eerie picture of a white goat with large horns pointing upwards a lifelike appearance as it caught the light from the street lamps. Espretha placed a hand on the heavy wooden door to The Goat. Before her fingers touched it, the door was yanked inwards. The elf jumped back as a large orc flew past us and landed in a brown, scummy puddle halfway across the street.

I raised my eyebrows. Normally The Goat was a welcome refuge for magical beings who were tolerated in everyday life and every so often needed a place to let it all hang loose without fear of the Magical Liaison Office being called up. The owner, a large troll named Goat, stepped outside. Outlined by the flickering torch effect lighting within, he looked more menacing than usual.

"No dealing tink here. You're barred!"

No wonder the owner was pissed. The fairy substance was highly addictive and highly illegal. Any inkling that The Goat was a drug front and the Magical Liaison Office would be on it like a shot. As the orc protested, holding one hand to his bruised head, Goat snapped a picture of the dealer with his smartphone and turned back to his establishment. He caught sight of Espretha and me standing to one side.

"Ladies," he gestured for us to go through the still-open door, "apologies for any unpleasantness, I won't have that fairy dust traded in my bar. Please accept a drink on the house." The troll stepped behind the ancient bar and took our orders.

As it was a free drink, I briefly considered trying some of the more exotic looking drinks lining the walls. There was a yellow bottle that seemed to have smoke coming from under the cork and a lot of twisted glassware containing coloured drinks that fizzed or changed colour as I looked at them. In the end I settled for something I knew I liked: vodka and cola for me. Espretha asked for a pint of ale. I looked at the elf, surprised at her order.

"What? We don't all drink sweet wine and mead you know. Just like dwarves don't all chug beer."

I took a sip of my own sweet drink to cover my embarrassment. "Sorry, er, I…"

My phone beeped, saving me from more awkward conversation. Lorandir wanting to know where I was. Espretha took in the olde worlde décor as I texted back that I was at The Goat but didn't mention I was with his former friend. He was still ignoring Espretha after she became part of a secret cult that awoke a dragon sleeping under Cardiff Castle. Another text message arrived. This one from Aloora asking how training went and where I was. Again I replied.

"You're popular," Espretha commented.

"Just some people wanting to know where I am."

"Lorandir?"

"And Aloora," I added hurriedly. I hadn't got round to telling Espretha I was dating her former friend and I wasn't sure how the deadly fighter would react.

"Must be nice to be cared for…" she was sounding wistful.

"Hey, it's not like everyone likes me. Most elves would rather I didn't exist," I tried to lighten the mood but winced when she met my gaze and made her next comment.

"I'll drink to that." We both took a swig of our beverages then she shifted her eyes away from mine and studied an ancient, blackened beam, "Any elves in particular?"

Schiztz. I didn't have a ready answer so decided to tell the truth, "Most of them actually…Lorandir's parents in particular."

She froze. I braced myself, one hand reaching back for the axe I still had strapped across my back. Then she started laughing. The musical sound caused a few heads to turn in our direction. I avoided the gazes of a couple of werewolves and finished my drink.

"I don't think it's that funny," I grumbled.

"No, it's just the thought of you meeting his mother," she started laughing again, "she's so stuck up and traditional and you're…" The elf gestured at me then wiped a tear of mirth from her perfect blue eyes. When she had finished laughing, she looked at me again, "So…you've met his parents?"

"Er, well his parents and a lot of the elves actually. I went to the King's memorial service."

She nodded tightly. I could sense her pain at not being able to attend an important elven ceremony. She acted tough. Schiztz. She was tough. But I knew she felt her exile from the elves keenly and it was worse because it was due to her own bad decisions.

"I can't believe I have to ask a dwarf this but…how was it?"

I shrugged and decided to continue with the honesty, "Weird. Really different to what I'm used to at a funeral. Very sedate. Respectful. Morthimas was crowned the new King and he's recruiting a new council."

She stared at me, "A new council?"

I nodded. It didn't seem that unusual to me that the new ruler would want some say in who was advising them.

"That's…"

"Unprecedented, I would say, but understandable given suspicions that some of the councillors might not have the elves' best interests at heart. Hi, I'm Aloora, nice to meet you properly," a familiar hand thrust into the space between us.

I blinked as I turned and looked into my friend's determined face. It hadn't occurred to me that she would come here. I jumped off the bar stool and stood staring between her and the elf "Er…"

Espretha looked like she had seen a ghost. Or maybe a more accurate description would be that she'd just seen the face of the victim she had kidnapped earlier in the year with the intention of forcing my gnomish friend to translate a ritual to raise a dzraking dragon. Yep that about covered the look on her face.

Chapter 11

"Hello Aloora…" Espretha stood up so quickly that her stool fell over. She stared at the small gnome before averting her eyes and studying the floor. I had never seen her look so uncomfortable and she'd once had her hand stuck in my underwear drawer. "Look I'm really sorry about the, you know, whole kidnapping thing. I…don't know what to say. I can't ever make it up to you…I should go."

She took a step towards the door but my friend grabbed her wrist. Espretha looked at the small hand circling her arm.

"You can start by buying me a drink and actually talking to me. A gin and tonic would be nice," sometimes my friend could be really stubborn.

"Yes, yes, of course," Espretha caught Goat's attention and gestured to our empty drinks adding an order for a gin and tonic for Aloora. The gnome slipped onto my seat and stared at the elf. Espretha righted her own stool and shifted uncomfortably. I pulled up another seat and sat tapping the bar nervously. Goat served the drinks and managed to lower the tension from boiling point to a milder simmer.

"Again, I'm really sorry."

"I know, and you've been exiled from Breconia and are being monitored by the Magical Liaison Office because of your part in the cult. I read your file," Aloora paused and looked directly into the elf's eyes, "So why did you do it?"

"I thought you'd read my file," Espretha took a long swig of her refilled pint.

"I want to hear it from you."

We all took another drink. My second vodka and cola was disappearing way too fast. I looked past my friends to the other end of the pub where a group of goblins were shrieking at each other as they adjusted bolts in scaffolding poles. Some sort of stage was being set up under the black beams.

"It all started with this elf, he was talking about having access to power that would boost our own magic. You don't know what it's like living in Breconia. There's so much back-biting and struggling for power and I was right in the centre of it, friends with the royal princes, even though I was from a common family."

"The file said you were adopted…"

My ears pricked up, and I swung my attention back to Espretha. This was all news to me. The elf nodded.

"The King and Queen thought they were being generous and they were. They gave me a place to live and I couldn't have asked for more. I tried to live up to their expectations, to make them proud but no matter what I did, I could never live up to Morthimas. The golden boy.

"Don't get me wrong, everyone was kind to me but they pitied me too. My magic wasn't as strong as any of theirs and

I wasn't adept at anything really, except fighting but that's not exactly prized. Everyone prefers archery to knives.

"Even with Lorandir, my best friend, sometimes the gap between us seemed insurmountable…So when an older elf started talking about power and respect, I decided to hear him out. It made a lot of sense at the time and there were plenty of others who believed him too.

"Over the course of a few months, I moved further and further away from my family and friends. And it all seemed normal. It got to the point where we'd report each other if we saw someone trying to contact their old friends. Then the leaders would take us to one side and explain again why what we were doing was right and how no one else could possibly understand.

"We were so focused on the ritual and seeking power. It was the only thing that mattered. So much so that I could justify the terrible things we did…even kidnapping you."

"You tried to talk to me, you weren't going to torture me."

The elf shrugged, "Maybe I wouldn't have tortured you but I might have stood by and let others do it."

Aloora shuddered and hugged herself. I placed a hand on her shoulder.

Espretha carried on, "I'm not proud of it. I'm not a nice person. I wanted to be powerful like Morty and Lorandir so much I used blood magic and now my magic is changed forever and I can't ever go back to my home. I deserve worse. I should be dead like the others." Bitterness crept into her voice but not self-pity.

"I didn't know you felt like that." I jumped at the familiar voice close to my ear. Damn elven light-footedness. I hadn't heard Lorandir approach us. I turned and saw my boyfriend standing behind us with Marco in his wake. Errol was coiled around his neck like a designer scarf and the human was staring at the faded signed photos of supernatural celebrities lining the walls. This was the first time he'd been in an all supernatural bar.

"How long have you been here?!" I was startled and it sounded ruder when I said it out loud.

"Long enough. You told me you were here, I thought I'd come find you and we could have a drink. I didn't know you'd be drinking with her." I shifted uncomfortably on the stool.

"Er…"

He put a reassuring hand on my knee, squeezing slightly to let me know he wasn't too upset. He turned back to Espretha, "I didn't know you felt like that around us. We always tried to include you."

"I know, but sometimes it felt like you were including me because you had to not because you wanted to. I was never fast enough or strong enough or powerful enough to keep up with you and the other noble borns. The cult offered me a way to find my own power, not be reliant on hand outs from the royal family."

"Why didn't you talk to me?"

Espretha shrugged again. Aloora answered instead.

"Brainwashing."

"What?"

“Classic cult. They brainwash you, keep you from friends and loved ones. She’s a victim here.” We all stared at the petite gnome. “I’m not saying what you did was right but it’s understandable I guess. Thank you for talking to me.”

The female elf raised her glass sarcastically, “Not a problem. If you ever want to hear about how much of an idiot I am, I’ll be happy to tell you.”

“Actually, I might have something else I need from you…I want to know how you awakened the dragon and more about the blood magic.”

I choked on my drink. Blood magic was no joke. It was the stuff of legends, and never the good ones. Something nudged the edge of my consciousness. My friend sighed and rolled her eyes at me, “For research purposes to help the Office. I’m not going to become a blood magician!” I caught my breath, relieved, and whatever thought that had been just out of reach disappeared.

Aloora turned back to the elf eagerly and began to ask more questions.

I looked around the pub, uneasy at the discussion of such dark power. The two attractive elves and Marco, who looked like an Italian model, were starting to draw attention to us. I didn’t like the way a shady individual who looked like a vampire was staring at Marco’s throat. I clocked a free table near the makeshift stage and suggested we move the conversation there.

I let Marco sit down first which meant his back was to the wall and he was furthest away from the other magical beings in the pub. I didn’t know how friendly they’d be towards a pure human. And surely it was only a matter of time before someone realised that's what he was.

The door opened, sending a stiff breeze into the bar and a vampire I recognised strode in talking over her shoulder to someone. I almost choked on my drink again when I saw it was Agent Jones and Maxi she was laughing with. Aloora noticed I was staring and turned to look while Marco patted me on the back as I continued to cough. Errol shifted and opened one of his amber eyes to give me a look of disdain at spoiling his perch. I tried not to feel annoyed that Errol felt more comfortable on Marco's broad shoulders than mine. Aloora waved the Magical Liaison Office agents over and they shouldered their way towards our table. I hadn't realised it had got so busy in here.

"What brings you here?" I didn't think I'd ever seen Agent Jones outside of the office. She looked strangely casual in jeans and a smart fitted top that hugged her curves.

Dot answered, shrugging off her jacket to reveal a knitted orange jumper, "I wouldn't miss the show!

"What show?"

"The supernatural drag show of course! It's opening tonight as a warm up for the main show at Blud next week. My friend's performing…in fact I'd better go find her." The vampire left her jacket on a chair and disappeared into the crowd. I took in the glitter and exaggerated make-up everyone else in the pub seemed to be wearing and felt very underdressed. If I'd have realised, I would have happily worn one of my corset tops and broken out the glitter eyeshadow I had shoved in the back of one of my drawers.

I offered to get the next round as Maxi sank into the vacant chair, "It's exciting what?! You know I once dressed in drag for my school play, the local paper said I was the best Cinderella they'd ever seen…I think I still have the dress."

At the bar, I felt eyes on me as I ordered. I turned and nearly hit a goblin who was staring at my chest. I frowned at him. I wasn't expecting a straight guy at a drag show. I took in the tight top and short shorts that verged on indecent and frowned some more. Then he opened his mouth, "That's some good make-up, fancy giving me some tips on how to look more feminine? Although I have to say the work out gear isn't working for you!" I gaped at him, unsure whether to be glad he'd said I looked feminine or upset that he thought I was a man.

"Er, I'm a woman…" Not the wittiest response.

The goblin's face turned into a mask of horror and his manner became instantly apologetic. I waved him away and turned quickly. Straight into a head height pair of rubber boobs. The tall wizard wearing them grunted, readjusted his low-cut top and straightened his beard.

"Watch out!"

I muttered my apologies and hurried back to the table with a tray of drinks.

"Keep it down human!" A voice growled from behind Maxi, who had started giving a falsetto performance of Shakespeare's Juliet, another one of his roles from school. I looked up…and up…and up into the scrunched up green face of an orc. He, or possibly she, was sporting pink diamantes across thick eyebrows and long pink fake eyelashes above a mouth that was painted with glitter. Pink, of course. A small wig balanced precariously on a large flat head. I wasn't sure what effect the orc was going for but if it was Miss Piggy on a really bad day, then they had nailed it. Maxi turned in his chair and held out a hand, "Yah will do, will do. Great eyelashes!"

The orc narrowed its eyes, which meant the huge eyelashes were now obscuring muddy yellow pupils. I swallowed and considered whether I'd need to get Bane out. Then Agent Jones downed her drink and stood up. The orc switched their gaze to the tall shifter.

"Is there a problem here?"

The orc contemplated an answer, taking in our table. Espretha already had a dagger balanced in one hand. Lorandir was gathering power to his palm. Not wanting to be left out, I brought Bane out from where I had stashed the axe under the table and rested it on my lap. Marco was trying to keep his cool composure as Errol growled softly near his ear. Aloora was trying to look menacing and had pulled a miniature crossbow from somewhere. It was pointed at the orc's nose. Maxi was still grinning at the orc with his hand out. Dot appeared suddenly next to Jones and smiled pointedly so her fangs were showing. The orc stared at Maxi then reached out and very gently shook his hand.

"Not a problem, I was just going to find a place to watch from over dere."

"Great idea, the acoustics will be much better from that side!" Maxi couldn't stop being the enthusiastic public school boy.

The rest of us relaxed as the orc moved away, shooting us ugly looks as they leaned against the bar. Although, to be fair, it wasn't like they could shoot us pretty looks with a face like that.

I was about to ask Maxi more about his acting career when the flame effect torches dimmed and the stage was lit by a spotlight floating near the ceiling. The platform was larger than I had expected, taking up a third of the space in the room. I took another look around the packed pub. There were more magical beings in here than I would have thought could fit in safely too. Magic was definitely screwing with the proportions of this place.

A petite figure with wings sashayed onto the stage. She was dressed in a nude bodysuit with leaves cascading over it to hide any unmentionables. Her breasts bounced as she made her way to the microphone.

As she reached the centre of the stage, the small figure leapt into the air and spun, sprinkling golden glitter from her hands in a cascade of light. I began to clap before realising I was the only one. I shrank back against my seat. The fairy flew to the top of the room, executed a somersault and then dived towards the floor before turning at the last second and landing on the stage in a full split. Everyone burst into applause at that. I winced as I brought my hands together. That had to hurt. Undeterred, the fairy used her wings to pull herself elegantly out of the splits and fly up to the microphone.

"Good evening ladies and gentlemen and things that go bump in the night. I am Titiana, Queen of the Fairies!"

There was more applause at that and a few laughs. The fairy smiled around the room and blew some more glitter into the crowd. Being near the front, some of it landed on our table, covering us all with a fine golden powder. I sneezed loudly as some of the glitter went up my nostrils.

"I thought the Queen of the Fairies was Tatiana?" I whispered to Aloora as I wiped my nose.

I couldn't see her eye roll in the dark room but I knew it was there, "Titty-Anna – it's a play on words. She's got huge…"

"Alright, alright, I get it!" I tried to force my eyes to stay on the fairy's attractive face but they kept wandering south to the enormous chest just below. I guessed that was the point.

"…Well we've got a treat in store for you tonight, let me tell you!"

More cheers.

"First up, from the dark countryside of Transylvania, please put your hands together for the incredible, the amazing, the talented…Count Dragula the camp-pire!"

Dot stood up and put her fingers in her mouth to wolf whistle the vampire that appeared from behind a velvet curtain. I guessed this was her friend. T

he vampire floated across the stage and gave air kisses to the small fairy. She was wrapped in a full black cloak sparkling with rhinestones so the only thing we could see was her huge bride of Frankenstein wig and appropriately vampy makeup. Music started and smoke began to fill the stage as the vampire started to move in time with the beat. She turned her back to the audience, lifted the cloak wide, showing us the bat shape of it before letting it fall to reveal a figure-hugging cat suit. She prowled around the stage, her red lips mouthing the words to the song. I settled back, enjoying the act.

The air above our table seemed to swirl and morph into purples and blues. For a second, I thought it was part of the act. The air curled and changed consistency, focused in a circle of power above us. We eyed each other, no one certain what was going on, and instinctively leant away from the centre of the table. Murmurs ruffled through the audience. This wasn't part of the show. A portal was opening directly above our table.

Chapter 12

Someone screamed. Other patrons started edging away. Goat groped under the bar for some type of weapon. To her credit, Count Dragula kept going with her act, shooting angry looks at our table as she shimmied around the stage.

A loud crack thundered through the room followed by something speeding out of the portal towards the table. I reacted fast and grabbed my drink. The thing hit the table hard and spilled the remaining glasses. It looked like a large stone, knobbly and round. As we watched, it unfurled itself into a small gargoyle. I groaned. I thought I recognised that leering face. It seemed like it recognised me too.

"'Ello gorgeous, aren't 'oo a sight for sore eyes"

"Gary! What the dzrak are you doing here?"

"Lookin' for 'oo! Well more specifically Agent Jones…" he turned in a slow shuffle in the middle of the table until he locked eyes with the lynx shifter. She was tapping her foot under the table and looked like she was about to explode. "…It's Mim. She sent me. Avalon is under attack."

"Right, come with us and explain."

Gary shook his head with some effort and grimaced, "No can do luv," Agent Jones' amber eyes narrowed dangerously and I swear her pupils started to morph into slits. A natural reaction to being called 'luv'. "I've gotta go to the elves next and the dwarves. This is big time sweetheart."

The beings nearest us had gone quiet. Those at the back were making disgruntled noises, annoyed at the interruption to the show. I saw Goat pushing his way towards the table. Agent Jones pinched the bridge of her nose in annoyance with the gargoyle. The portal still swirled above our table, adding an eerie lighting effect to the pub.

The large troll owner reached our table but before he could speak, Agent Jones held up her hand to silence him.

"Right, give me five seconds!" Goat blinked in shock as the shifter pushed her way past him and through the throng until she found someone who she grabbed by the shoulder and brought back to our table. It was a young wizard wearing a black top covered with rhinestone stars. He blinked his kohl-rimmed eyes at us, wide with fear, as he approached. "This is Smith, one of our wizards. He's going to cast a silence shield so only we can hear what Gary says next and the lovely Dragula can get on with her show, that alright with you Goat?" Agent Jones gave a small wave to the vampire on stage as Goat nodded dazedly. Count Dragula's eyes were glowing red and her smiles were getting a lot toothier as the interruption continued. The shifter nudged Smith, "Well, get on with it!"

The wizard was nervous but he mumbled the spell and soon we were encased in an invisible bubble. It distorted the world outside our table a little and silence fell as the barrier made sure the music didn't get through and what we said stayed inside. Through the refracted air, I watched as Goat made his way back to the bar. Count Dragula was now gyrating to a different beat.

"What's going on?" Agent Jones levelled a stare at the small gargoyle. He scratched his ear and began talking.

"Well, Mim had jus' bin visiting Omensford when she feels this attack see. She rushes back and boom, there's these dark elves trying to get into Avalon." Aloora let out a gasp of shock but Gary carried on, "We wasn't too worried at first. Y'know 'ow strong the defences are. Anyways then fings start to get dicey. Dark elves breached the first defences and now they're at the last ward, so she sends me to get some 'elp. And 'ere I am."

The other supernatural beings and Maxi looked at each other in horror.

"So, she sed to give 'oo this," Gary held out one clawed hand with a small bead in it. Agent Jones reached for it and held it up to examine it. Her face looked eerie in the purplish glow it emitted. Unreadable gold lettering swirled over its surface.

Gary flexed his small wings, "Anyways no rest for the wicked," he gave us a wink, "if someone could give me a boost…" He gestured to the portal still crackling above our heads.

Maxi leaned forward and nearly fell onto the table when he tried to lift the small, but heavy, gargoyle. Dot waved him off and picked up the stocky creature with the ease of someone who had supernatural strength. She tested his weight and stuck her tongue out slightly as if she was doing some mental arithmetic before she threw him into the portal.

We all looked up. His shape seemed to elongate for a split second before it disappeared and the portal closed with a burst of silvery light. It was strangely quiet in the silent bubble. Then Agent Jones barked an order.

"Right, we're going to Avalon. To the Office to tool up," she stomped out of the bubble, popping it as she passed through. She cleared the way to the door, barging into several members of the audience on the way out. They took one look at the bad temper etched on her face and stepped aside. The rest of us followed in her wake, careful not to make eye contact. Dot turned just before we left and gave a thumbs up to Count Dragula who was leaving the stage. I heard Titiana announce the next act – The Banshees – and saw a flash of blonde hair before the wailing started and we left the pub.

Jones marched us to the Magical Liaison Office headquarters on the other side of the city centre. The pace was too fast for me to speak the questions swirling around my mind so I saved them up for when we arrived. We approached the discreet black door that marked the Magical Liaison Office and Agent Jones held up a pass to a slender brass plaque.

I stamped my feet to keep out the chill of the evening air as I looked around. The Office was sandwiched between a four-storey grey house that had been converted into offices and a run-down church. There were several panes missing from the old stained glass windows and some fresh graffiti adorned the brick wall next to a badly spelled message telling magic users to go back home. I squinted as I tried to make out what I was looking at before my brain processed the image. Not classy. And not anatomically correct either.

The beeping and buzzing from behind the brass panel stopped and the black door opened inwards. We all trooped inside, Dot's heels clacked on the tiled floor. I was glad I was in my gothic-style boots as the shiny tiles were slippery even when dry. We walked past abstract paintings in muted colours and several closed doors.

Dot slipped off downstairs with the two elves to the space that I knew from experience held a garage and a training area complete with weapons. Agent Jones led us to a maroon-coloured wooden door, slightly at odds with the modern interior. There was an ugly brass door knocker in the shape of a face stuck to the door. The ears were asymmetrical and too large for its face and its mouth was turned down with deep, creased wrinkles etched into its cheeks on either side.

A brass ring hung from an upturned nose. It appeared to be sleeping. Agent Jones pummelled the door with her fist whilst lifting the ring and letting it fall. The knocker woke up. The first thing it saw was Agent Jones' pass shoved into its face. It blinked.

"What's the rush? I thought you'd all gone home…" the knocker trailed off as it took in the shifter's bad mood. "Alright, alright, I'm opening." It took in the rest of us, "Are they all coming in too?"

"Yep," Agent Jones was already through the door.

“Where’s their passes? I’ve got to see their passes!” The knocker’s voice was nasal and petulant and the door began to swing shut.

“Emergency protocol.”

“But….”

“Let them in Fred!”

The door knocker mumbled to itself and its eyes began to glow a dull red, but the door stayed open and we all pressed inside. Marco was the last one through and the door swung shut with an ominous thud behind him.

The room we entered was shaped sort of like a pentagon, if a pentagon had strange angles that didn’t quite add up. A large television set took up most of the wall that the door was set into. It was off.

Bookshelves holding huge leather-bound volumes lined three of the walls. Aloora made a beeline for these and starting pulling old texts out onto the antique carpet that covered the floor. Agent Jones headed straight for the fourth wall where a fire burned in an enormous fireplace. Above the marble mantelpiece hung an armoury of ancient weapons.

I watched with my mouth open as Agent Jones balanced on a chair and selected several swords and guns. She forced them all into her fake crocodile skin handbag, muttering to herself as she did so. Marco gaped as he took it all in and he staggered into a small wooden desk. The laptop and green angle poise lamp perched on it wobbled slightly but they didn’t fall off. I patted him on the shoulder. I had felt the same way when I first entered the room. I didn’t mention the secret door to the kitchen behind one of the bookshelves.

Maxi headed to his own desk and pulled out some silver metal boxes. He adjusted a few settings and then tucked them under one of his arms before retrieving a duffel bag from under the desk. Suitably loaded, he went to help Aloora carry her growing pile of books. I spotted a pair of sunglasses on a small table that were emitting a familiar magical aura. I picked them up and put them on.

They worked exactly like my enchanting goggles back in my workshop. I could see the auras of magical beings through the tinted lenses. Aloora glowed a bright violet while Dot was a dull red figure. I took them off and the auras disappeared from sight.

They were a bit more practical than carrying my steampunk style goggles around with me so I hooked them onto the neck of my t-shirt. I decided the most useful thing I could do was help Aloora so I picked up a volume of *The Myths of Avalon* that weighed more than Errol, grabbed my friend's own go-bag stashed under her desk and rested it on the back of one of the comfy leather sofas that were set in front of the fire as I waited for some orders.

Agent Jones had finished checking her bag and she raised her head to look at us, "Ready?"

Aloora and Maxi nodded and, with mine and Marco's help, hefted a large amount of books to the door. It took several blows from Agent Jones and a threat to melt him down for Fred to open up and let us out. He yawned theatrically as we went through, "Sorry, I must have been asleep."

Agent Jones gave him a look and we headed down to the garage. The doors of the grey van were thrown open and weapons were piled up inside. I recognised the swords I had crafted for the team earlier in the year with fire and ice enchantments woven into their metal blades. A number of crossbows and other weapons lay across the swords creating an arsenal inside of the van. Agent Jones gave it a cursory nod. I briefly wondered why the weapons weren't strapped securely to the inside of the van.

Aloora motioned for me to put the books and her bag on top of the pile of sharp blades. I did so carefully and stepped back. As I stepped into the van, the reason why the weapons were piled up became clear. The usual weapons slots were already filled with knives, what looked like a pair of scimitars and more crossbows. This might be the most lethal van in all of Cardiff tonight.

Maxi climbed into the front seat alongside Agent Jones who had claimed the driver's seat and was passing her handbag to Maxi to hold. The elves were already in the van, seatbelts done up. Espretha was spinning one of her daggers in her hand nervously. Lorandir gave me a tight smile and I went to sit next to him, settling against the multi-coloured knitted throw that covered the seat.

Aloora and Marco sat at the back. Marco had a dazed expression on his face as if he couldn't quite believe what was happening but he seemed to be going with the flow. Agent Jones hadn't said anything about him being here, so I guessed it was alright. Errol sensed the tense atmosphere and crawled over to sit on my lap, where I stroked him reassuringly as he nervously blew smoke rings from his nostrils.

I heard the back doors slam shut and Dot climbed in and claimed one of the free places. The throw covering her seat was a sea of greens and blues in contrasting stripes. She grinned and gave us a thumbs up. I tried to smile back, but I knew it looked taut and fake. Agent Jones revved the engine. The noise reverberated around the enclosed garage. She looked at Maxi and nodded. He brought out one of the silver boxes and held it up then studied the small bead that Gary had given us. He tapped something into the box and held it in outstretched arms towards the windscreen.

With a sucking swooshing sound, a portal appeared just beyond the windscreen. It was large enough to fit a person through and shimmered in opalescent colours. Maxi swore and adjusted the settings. The portal grew until it was large enough for a small lorry to pass through, taking up the full space of the garage. He pressed another combination of buttons on the box's sleek silver side and the portal began to move away from us. It made me queasy to watch as the surface of the portal rippled and moved away. When it reached the far wall, Maxi stopped and nodded to Agent Jones. She slammed the van into gear, revved the engine and accelerated hard towards the swirling surface. We were on our way to Avalon.

Chapter 13

I gripped Lorandir's hand tightly as we entered the portal. There was a strange sucking sensation and my vision swam with small rainbows. I felt like I was falling forwards and sideways at the same time, like a strange sort of vertigo. My stomach lurched. I was not a fan of portal travel.

We exited the portal onto a cobbled road. The van bumped along as its tyres connected with the uneven surface, adding travel sickness to my vertigo. The vehicle swerved sharply as Agent Jones avoided a tree where the road turned. My stomach protested sharply as the van pulled to a sharp stop. Where on earth were we?

"Good job Dan," muttered Dot. It looked like she patted the metal interior with her slender hand.

"Dan?" Espretha's voice was too loud in the muffled silence of this realm.

"Dan the van," Dot shrugged.

I heard Agent Jones swear before starting the van again and moving more slowly this time. We were in a dark forest, the trees so densely packed that we couldn't even see a glimpse of sky as we drove along. The headlights illuminated gnarled trees stretching on either side of the road. Occasionally, strange fae creatures would dart across our path. One animal that looked like a giant white stag bared pointed teeth at us as the headlights paralysed it in the middle of the worn road. Agent Jones beeped the horn and it bounded off with an enormous leap back into the undergrowth.

I experimented with the sunglasses I had taken. The pink auras of fae creatures filled my vision in every direction. Small bird shaped auras stretched their wings in the trees. Cat-sized animals stalked through the undergrowth, invisible to the naked eye. One large shape that reminded me of a hippopotamus loomed to our left before heading slowly back away from the road. I took the glasses off again quickly. It was unnerving knowing so many animals were surrounding us in the forest. I stroked Errol absently to try to calm myself. The small wyrm flexed his wings, relaxing. Then he sank his claws into my leg and started growling.

"Ouch! Dzrak it all Errol!"

Everyone stared at me. We had been silent, which had added to the creepiness of the forest. My shout of pain broke the tension and Marco laughed nervously.

Agent Jones twisted sharply in her seat, "What is he doing here?"

I was surprised. I thought Jones didn't mind my pet wyrm tagging along, "I couldn't exactly leave him at the Office…" I started before I tailed off. Jones wasn't looking at me. She was glaring at Marco, seated at the back and holding Aloora's hand. No one spoke.

"We have to get him back. It's not safe. Maxi, open a portal."

The other human shook his head, "Sorry to say I don't think this has got enough juice and the other one is only a back-up. I don't want to risk it conking out on us too. Maybe Madam Mim can help, yah?"

Agent Jones pinched the bridge of her nose and opened her mouth to say something.

Marco screamed and pointed out of the windscreen. We followed his terror-stricken gaze. Agent Jones slammed on the brakes and the van screeched to a stop in front of a creature I couldn't have imagined in my worst nightmares, although I suspected it was going to feature in them for a long time from now on.

The creature looked like a cross between a horse and a large dog. If both of those things were the spawn of demons. And the size of a train carriage. And had four eyes instead of two. The dog-like head opened its mouth to reveal rows of jagged teeth. It roared at the van. The sound was partway between a scream and a howl and all the way terrifying. Flecks of spittle landed on the windscreen. The automatic wipers started. This enraged the creature and its pointed ears lay back flat against its head as it reared up on its hooved back legs.

Agent Jones thumped the gearstick into reverse and took us back along the bumpy path. The monster's huge dog-like forepaws hit the ground exactly where the engine would have been. Enraged, it roared again. I watched with horror as it started chasing us. Agent Jones suddenly had a crossbow in hand and the window open. She managed to let off a crossbow bolt. It hit the creature in one of its glowing green eyes.

Maxi and Dot followed suit, aiming out of their own windows. Blood trickled from the monster's ear as another bolt found its mark. The thing screamed in pain. Then it sat back on its haunches and let off a long, low howl. The sound echoed among the trees. Until I realised it wasn't an echo. It was more howls.

Three more creatures bounded out from the forest behind the van. We were surrounded. Agent Jones pulled the van to a stop and revved the engine. It was the strangest game of chicken I'd ever seen. The dog/horse monsters growled and bared their teeth, pacing around the van. The first one slunk towards us, showing its fangs. It took its time, savouring the kill.

"I need this van on fire in three…two…"

I realised Agent Jones was speaking to me. Belatedly I unbuckled my seatbelt and crouched on the floor, searching for the fire rune I had etched into the floor of the van. My questing fingers found it and I activated the rune with the Dwarfish word for fire just after Agent Jones got to "one!"

She released the handbrake and we squealed forward. Straight at the creature. Its eyes closed against the blaze of flame, too bright in this dark forest. It staggered to one side with shock and we scraped past. I felt a thud as the van collided with its flank. The smell of burning leather flooded in through the vents. The creature shrieked in pain and rolled away from the flames.

The vehicle continued to judder over the ancient road as Jones put her foot down. More howls sounded around us. They were chasing us. The van was heating up. I heard Lorandir activate the shields on his own sword and on my ancestral axe, which he slid along the floor towards me. I jumped back to avoid being cut by my own blade. The axe sailed under the front seat, shield still activated. The fire began to die down now I wasn't channelling my own power into sustaining the rune.

One of the monsters had caught up to the van and was running alongside. Its pink tongue lolled from its mouth and saliva fell from its mouth in long dribbling tendrils. Dot aimed her crossbow out of the window and let off a bolt straight into its maw. It stumbled to one side, keening as it died. The creatures kept pace with us but seemed wary to approach now two of the pack's members had been injured. Lorandir sent a bolt of power into a third and the monsters disappeared into the forest with a yelp. I allowed the fire to continue for a further minute until I was sure I couldn't hear the sound of panting following us through the forest of nightmares. Then I extinguished it and the only light left was the dull glow of the van's headlights as we continued into the night.

Agent Jones kept the vehicle going as fast as she could, determined to get us away from the forest and towards wherever it was this road was taking us. I climbed back into my seat and refastened my seatbelt, trying not to think of what else might be hiding in the trees.

A pinpoint of white light appeared on the horizon. I stared at it. Then we were clear of the forest. The sky opened up above us in strange streaks of blues, purples and greens, illuminating the open plain in eerie colours. The sky seemed to hum with magic.

A strange purple net stretched above us, getting closer. As my vision cleared, I realised it was a ward and we were heading straight for it. As I drew breath to shout a warning, Agent Jones brought the van to a squealing halt. The force of the van stopping threw me forward and Errol growled in protest as he was nearly thrown from my lap. My heart was thudding in my chest as I took in our surroundings.

"Aurora Borealis!" Maxi breathed. The northern lights. Caused by particles hitting the magical energy fields surrounding the earth. Except we weren't on earth anymore. We were in the fae realm. The magic here was concentrated and the ethereal lights stretched as far as the eye could see, flashing against the starry night sky. The dark stone road led straight through the ward.

Behind its translucent surface, dark shapes were visible against the magical sky, too blurred for me to make them out. The ward must be strong to be visible and I wondered who had created it and what they were protecting. Or who they were trying to keep out. I shuddered involuntarily.

"Right. This is Avalon and Mim is holed up behind that ward." As we looked, the ward rippled and shuddered before resuming its more solid appearance. "It's under attack and we need to help. Maxi, Dot, get us in."

Maxi swallowed and clutched the small purple bead to his chest. He looked around at the unfamiliar landscape before stepping cautiously out of the van. I noticed he had armed his standard issue Magical Liaison Office crossbow and was holding it with his free hand. Dot had her own crossbow which she was holding, safety off, ready to fire. Her other hand held the ice sword she had grabbed from the back of the van. She spoke the Dwarfish word for ice and activated its rune. Instantly the sword crackled and a sheet of ice covered the blade. I allowed myself a moment of pride at my work.

Maxi sprinted towards the ward. Dot kept pace with him easily. Her head swivelled from side to side as she scanned the surroundings for more monsters. At the ward, Maxi held the bead aloft and touched it to the purplish net. He traced a shape and a gap appeared in the protection spell. He kept the bead connected to the ward and motioned for us to get through. Agent Jones drove up carefully. I heard the shriek of the metal roof scraping along the ward as she edged the van through the space. Once inside, Dot sprinted through, keeping her crossbow aimed out of the hole. Maxi stepped over the threshold and pulled the bead away from the spell. The gap closed instantly. I noticed Maxi was shaking as he got back into the van.

"Good job everyone. Welcome to Avalon."

Chapter 14

Agent Jones drove us along the bumpy road for another couple of minutes, heading towards an open gate in a white stone wall that stretched out to either side as far as I could see. Inside the wall were small huts made from wood with thatched rooves. The headlights revealed shuttered windows and no movement. But then, it was the middle of the night. The flickering northern lights gleamed off a large white castle just past an open square. I fought to keep my eyes open.

The adrenaline that had coursed through me while we had been driving through the sinister forest was fading and the alcoholic drinks I'd imbibed were telling me I needed sleep. I did a long blink and then snorted as we pulled to a stop just outside the keep. My body ached from the long, jarring journey in a vehicle with what could only be called dodgy suspension. I forced my eyes open. Handing Errol to Lorandir, I waited until everyone else was out before digging under the front seat for my axe. I found it by slicing open my finger on one of its razor-sharp blades and felt more cautiously for the handle. I retrieved the axe, stepped out of the van and holstered the weapon across my back before stretching. Errol was already asleep, curled around the elf's neck.

Madam Mim was standing by a large wooden door. She held a lantern that reflected oddly off her face, making her look old and tired. A complete contrast to the elegant woman I'd met less than a year ago.

"Thank goodness you came, please come in."

Mim led the way through the door and into a courtyard. There were tents and makeshift shelters set up like a refugee camp. The lamp reflected off sad eyes as fae creatures huddled together under blankets. Small fires provided scant heat for the poor magical beings.

We hurried past and into the castle itself. There was a large great hall with a fire burning low. Here there were families clustered in small bunches throughout the room. I heard a baby cry and the quick "hush, hush" of a mother trying to quiet it. I tried not to stare at the fae families with their large eyes and bright skin. One small boy stared as we passed, his horns catching the light from the fire as he blinked back tears. Instead, I let my eyes wander upwards, taking in the arching beams, across tapestries of knights and dragons, and up to the painted shields that lined the wall.

Mim led us through this room, along a narrow corridor and into another space, smaller and more intimate than the great hall.

A group of five women were sitting on antique sofas, sipping tea by the soft firelight. One of them was doing something complicated with a crochet hook as she worked with a ball of yarn. The string of pearls around her neck gleamed softly in the warm glow of the fire.

Mim strode over to the large stone fireplace where two huge dogs were sleeping on a rug. They looked like a cross between a corgi and a wolf, cute in a fierce sort of way. Mim patted one of the dogs on its head as it opened its chocolate brown eyes and stoked up the fire that was laid in the stone fireplace.

She added some words of magic so it flared quickly, lighting up the sitting room. Sparks from the fire travelled out and into the room, heading for tall beeswax candles that sat in large candelabras on every surface. The candles had artful blobs of melted wax running down them, creating a well-used effect. They looked like they belonged on a movie set. I watched the one closest to me. It was set into a spiralling metal candlestick and I noticed that although it burned brightly, the candle itself never seemed to get any lower.

Maxi strode over to the ladies and offered each of them his hand, "Maximillian Baskerville! Pleasure to meet you what!"

"Interesting use of the word pleasure young man," one of the women replied with a purr in her voice. Maxi's cheeks flushed and he stepped back behind Agent Jones.

One of the ladies rose and offered Mim her seat. She slumped onto an armchair with a murmured "Thank you," and rubbed her eyes. If we were tired, she looked exhausted. Dark bags stretched under her usually bright eyes and her jet black hair now sported glimmers of white. With a motion of her arm, more seats appeared in the room. The five women didn't flinch at the appearance of sofas from mid-air and lifted their feet genteelly as their own settees scraped across the floor to make room for ours.

Mim gestured at the empty seats and we sank into them gratefully. The corgis roused themselves from the fire and ambled over to sniff at Mim's guests. I brushed away the tan and white one that jumped up and tried to lick my face, coming away from the encounter covered in drool. Errol growled at the black corgi that tried to investigate the wyrm sleeping around my boyfriend's neck. It was persistent and after two more attempts, managed to sweep its lolling tongue over the wyrm's back.

Errol responded by digging his claws into Lorandir and breathing a small flame at the dog. The corgi backed down and ambled over to where Marco sat on the floor, leaning against the arm of a small sofa. He allowed the corgis to lick his face before they settled down next to him.

"The wish hounds like you," Mim commented as she sat up in her chair.

"Wish 'ound?" Marco's Italian accent sounded thick against the new words.

Mim nodded, "They are great protectors and my mounts in battles."

I looked again at the large dogs. They were big but they didn't look big enough to carry a person, even one as slender as Madam Mim. I was about to ask about them when Agent Jones got right down to business.

"What's occurring Mim?"

"Mostrim. Dark elves. Here of all places."

"Why didn't you call us for help sooner?"

"I thought they'd been destroyed…"

"Just hiding," everyone turned to look at me and I coughed, "er, well this kobold told me they'd gone into hiding."

"And you didn't think to tell anyone?" The oldest lady peered through her large spectacles at me with sparkling eyes. She sounded curious and at the same time like she was telling me off. She reminded me of my grandmother, maybe women get to a certain age and suddenly they can do that voice.

"I, er, wasn't sure whether to believe her," I thought back to the surly kobold, Bethan, who'd told me that dark elves had burned down my shop. She didn't exactly give off trustworthy vibes.

"Fine. Well that ties in with what I've found too. They've been infiltrating organisations everywhere, the MLO, I mean Magical Liaison Office, included. I ousted our Director a couple of months ago but it looks like this was their game plan." Agent Jones stated matter of factly. I blinked at her. The other members of the Magical Liaison Office didn't look shocked. I guessed this was old news to them but it would be nice if sometimes my best friend told me something about her work that wasn't dragon related.

Marco raised his hands, "Why are they attacking 'ere? Why not somewhere on…earth? We're not in Wales anymore are we?"

He did well to keep the panic from showing in his voice but I saw his adam's apple bob up and down as he swallowed.

Madam Mim held his gaze, "Avalon is more than a physical place. This realm is connected to everything good in all worlds. If it should fall, then it will be easier for them to take over everywhere else. Hope will be gone you see and without that, no one will fight."

"Hope?"

"When Pandora opened the box from the gods that contained all the evils of humanity, hope fluttered out too. My mothers decided to protect it and so they brought it to this realm - the very centre of all worlds, connected to everything. They weaved it into the very fabric of this place and let it flow to light even the darkest of places. Hope is the reason all of us strive for a better life and because of that there have been fabulous innovations…

"Avalon was once a court with representation from all sentient races. Bold warriors who were the champions of their people. We sat in the great hall at a round table so none would be higher than the others and we tried to create peace, but there was one who refused. He broke from us and in his exile founded a new race.

"Sons and daughters of discord, enemies of hope, their aim was to expand and colonise every realm and so they made themselves enemies of all. Great wars were fought with many alliances founded and eventually the dark elves were destroyed.

"But they had sowed enough mistrust that many races could not stand to uphold the old alliances. Many of the members of the court were killed and we disbanded long ago and I have guarded this realm, keeping it safe. It is a refuge for all who still hope but now, if it goes…" Madam Mim broke into a choking sob.

My thoughts spiralled. Was this why elves and dwarves didn't get along? And why mundane humans mistrusted magical beings? I rubbed my temples. This was a lot to take in.

"That's not going to happen. Enough of the history lesson, what do we know?" Agent Jones was all business.

A tall man stepped from the shadows in the corner of the room. He wore a white and gold tabard that fell to his knees. It might have been in fashion during the Middle Ages and somehow it suited him. His close-cut greying beard and the hard look in his blue eyes leant him an air of authority. At his hip I saw a jewelled scabbard and a sword that seemed familiar.

"They hath chosen their time well. The Winter Solstice is when the power of Avalon is at its weakest. They seemeth to be concentrating their attack at one spot in the ward, hoping to weaken it there rather than spread their forces more thinly. We hath scouts monitoring the situation. They report a large force and not only dark elves but others too who have joined their cause. They hath several bands of trolls, ogres and two giants as well as a troupe of goblins and an ifrit. We estimate that there are near fifty thousand of them in total."

I gulped and forgot about the sword. Fifty thousand. What the dzrak?! This wasn't an attack. This was a war.

"How long will the ward hold?"

"We have as long as Mim and Merlin can carry on regenerating it."

I looked at the exhausted sorceress slumped on the chair. I didn't know where Merlin was but I didn't think we had long.

A pounding rhythm beat through my head. I rubbed my temples. It didn't help. Then I realised that the rhythm wasn't internal. It was drums. Nearby.

Agent Jones heard them too and leapt up, her crossbow out. She ran back through the main hall. Nobody spoke as we waited for her, but we all sat more upright, hands clutching our weapons.

The drumming stopped abruptly. The door burst open. Everyone was on their feet, weapons drawn. I held Bane tightly, the adrenaline keeping me upright. The innocent looking women's hands glowed as they gathered power behind us. Witches.

Agent Jones stepped in, followed by two heavily-armoured dwarves. One of them was carrying a huge war hammer as large as he was. Jones arched an eyebrow as she took in our fighting stances. Madam Mim shook her hands to get rid of the power she had been drawing and glided over to greet the newcomers. She bent and grasped their forearms in the traditional Dwarfish greeting.

"Thank goodness you've come!"

The shorter of the dwarves stepped forward, rested the haft of his war hammer on the ground and removed his helmet. I recognised Master Ironfist, a member of the Dwarven Arms Council.

"Greetings all. We have brought two thousand of our finest warriors to aid Avalon." He surveyed the room and took in the group of women who had sank back down onto their sofas and were now passing a packet of biscuits round. "Where is the war council being held?"

Agent Jones met his eyes, "This is it."

To his credit, Ironfist hid his disappointment reasonably well by coughing into his long, neat beard. His reply was interrupted by Gary the gargoyle popping into the room. A bluish black portal closed behind him.

"Wotcha ev'ryone!" He looked around at our faces and grinned at Mim, "I dun wot 'oo asked me."

A single piercing note from some type of horn broke into the shock of having a small gargoyle leer at us. Lorandir and Espretha both stood and exchanged glances. Agent Jones jerked her head towards the door, indicating that they should go. The elves had arrived.

Morthimas strode into the room, tall and striking in golden lacquered armour. He seemed more regal than the unsure elf I had spoken to just last week, as if kingship had settled on him overnight. I rubbed my eyes and tried to stay focused as he greeted the room.

He nodded courteously at the dwarven representatives and then kissed Madam Mim's hand gallantly. This caused her to give a wry smile which made her seem a little like her old self. Lorandir and Espretha entered behind him and retook their seats.

One of the ladies whispered to another, "Say what you like about the elves, they are easy on the eyes."

"I bet that's not all they're easy on…" replied a tanned lady with red lipstick suggestively.

"And you ladies are…?" The tips of Morthimas' ears had turned pink but he managed to sound suitably courteous and disinterested at the same time.

The eldest lady stood and answered, “We are members of the Omensford Witches’ Institute…” the speaker was elbowed in the thigh by a woman next to her, “I mean to say, the Omensford Witches, Wizards and Warlocks’ Institute, an inclusive organisation for all magical beings, your highness.” She executed a small curtsey and sat back down, huffing to herself, “Although I still don’t see why we had to change the name…”

Agent Jones stepped into the middle of the room, “Now we’ve got the introductions out of the way, perhaps we can plan a strategy?”

Chapter 15

Madam Mim conjured a large table with a three dimensional map of Avalon spread over it. The map was exceptionally detailed and I thought I even spotted our van parked outside the castle walls. The castle itself loomed tall and bright in the centre of the table. The man in the old-fashioned tabard pointed out where the enemy was clustered against the ward and shadows appeared on the map as he described the army. I shuddered as I saw the giants and the ifrit loom large on the table. I had never seen either in person and had no desire to change that any time soon.

Agent Jones took charge and barked questions at the man who looked like a medieval knight. To his credit, he answered quickly and calmly. Morthimas chimed in with his own questions, wanting to know about the mounts that the besiegers had.

As Agent Jones and the others began to plan a battle strategy, I sank into my chair. This was surreal. And I started to feel powerless and afraid. I rubbed my head to try to clear the unwelcome thoughts from my mind. My eyes were heavy and after some long blinks, I fell asleep. My dreams were full of fighting and then a fiery ifrit with horns stretching as tall as trees roared in my face. I woke up in a sweat and looked around. We were still in the sitting room.

Agent Jones tapped her foot against the floor, "Right everyone. Get some sleep. Tomorrow we fight."

I checked my phone to hide the embarrassment of falling asleep. It was three a.m. Madam Mim opened the carved wooden door and spoke into the dark corridor. Instantly several small sprites appeared with bright blue skin and beating wings.

"Follow them to your rooms. The least I can offer you is beds for the night."

I moved slowly along a corridor that seemed as if it was carved from white marble. Smokeless torches lit our way from evenly spaced sconces in the walls. The flickering light caught on seams of purplish crystals embedded in the stone walls.

Every so often we passed a picture or a tapestry that depicted a historic scene. They wouldn't have looked out of place in any castle in the human world, except that the people and creatures depicted were definitely fae. A man and a woman with the ears and horns of deer stared out of one picture and in another tapestry, a white unicorn nuzzled a red-skinned woman with wings sprouting delicately from her back. In the torchlight, I could imagine the figures were moving.

I thought of the soldiers the elves and dwarves had brought and looked out of the arrow slit windows as we were led up a tower to our rooms. There were tents pitched outside the castle walls and bright fires lit for warmth. I guessed they were alright.

My feet were heavy as we climbed the stairs but eventually the small sprite stopped and gestured to a heavy wooden door. It opened smoothly at my touch, as if by magic. Which I supposed it was. We said goodnight to the others and stepped inside as they continued on to their own rooms.

When Lorandir and I were finally alone in our room, I kicked off my boots and my workout gear, letting them pool onto the thick carpet. I sank onto the soft four poster bed, too tired to take in the wooden carvings of strange winding vines that snaked up the bedframe. I closed my eyes, shutting out the woven emerald drapes that surrounded the bed.

But I found I couldn't sleep. A wave of desperation and fear rolled through me, and I curled into a foetal position, overwhelmed. Errol slunk off to curl up close to the fire that burned in the stone fireplace. I felt the bed sink as Lorandir lay down next to me.

I opened my eyes, gazing into his and reached out to stroke his face. Even tired, he still looked gorgeous. Sometimes it just wasn't fair.

"So what's the plan?"

"Basically…try not to die."

I considered that, "Sounds like a dzraking good plan to me."

I moved towards him and pressed my mouth to his in a hungry kiss. If this was our last night alive together, I wanted to savour every moment. He returned my kiss passionately as if he knew what was going through my mind. His hands skimmed my skin as if he wanted to memorise every inch of me. We made love fast and desperately, clinging to each other, trying to say everything we couldn't say in words. Afterwards, I fell asleep in his arms, my head tight against his chest, listening to his strong heart beat while he stroked my hair.

Chapter 16

The morning came too soon. Dawn's rosy fingers clawed across the land impatiently. I awoke groggily with a gnawing sense of dread knotting my stomach. It took me a second to remember where we were. And then the dread made sense. I tightened my grip around my lover's body. He kissed the top of my head.

"Come on, we're going to be late."

As simple as if we were going to meet a friend for breakfast. I got dressed slowly, trying to delay the inevitable battle. We were both quiet as we checked our weapons and prepared to leave the room. I strung Bane to my back. Its weight felt both comforting and disturbing. Lorandir strapped on his sword, doing up the thick leather belt carefully. It felt like we were forest animals forced to leave the comfort of our den. I dragged my feet as we made our way to the great hall. My heavy boots scuffed along the stone steps.

Inside the great hall, the families had moved to make way for tables and a huge cauldron was bubbling on a large fire. The women from the Omensford Witches' Institute were standing beside it dishing up something that looked like porridge into bowls for a queue of people. In the light I was able to take in their modern clothing compared to the leather jerkins the fae creatures who called Avalon their home were wearing for protection. Lorandir went over to them muttering something about seeing if they had any bows.

I made my way to the far end of one of the trestle tables that now lined the hall. I sank onto one of the low benches and leaned on the wooden table, hunching my shoulders. I didn't want to talk to anyone. Lorandir took a seat opposite me and plonked two wooden bowls full of grey porridge in front of us.

For once, I wasn't hungry. I used the pewter spoon to stir the food aimlessly. It was something to do. The table emptied slowly, leaving us alone. Espretha entered the room hesitantly. She grabbed a bowl and caught my eye before choosing a seat at the very end of the table. Alone. I was about to ask her to come over when Aloora and Marco joined us, carrying their own bowls of food.

"Something you said?" my friend asked, her voice a little too casual and a pitch higher than she normally spoke.

I looked around at the empty table and forced a smile, "Nah, they just didn't want to hear about your latest dragon research!"

She playfully punched my arm before raising a spoonful of steaming oats to her mouth, "Not bad."

"I thought you were going home Marco?"

He shook his head ruefully, "It is too unstable to open a portal, they say. So I will stay here in the castle. It will be safe?"

I turned back to my bowl, avoiding the question. The rest of the Magical Liaison Office team walked into the room, providing a welcome distraction. Agent Jones was exchanging words with Morthimas and Ironfist, heads bent together as they discussed the upcoming battle.

The three of them looked bright-eyed and ready for anything. Agent Jones was wearing leather armour that fit her perfectly. The dwarf had chainmail covered by a breastplate and was holding a sturdy helmet under one arm. He laid his huge war hammer against a wall and laughed at something as he took the bowl of porridge he was offered.

Morthimas' armour was more ornate, as befitted a king I supposed, with the royal crest embossed on his gleaming breastplate. It seemed to be made from a highly polished lacquer over leather with golden metal filigree covering the wooden surface. It looked like the first time the armour had been worn into battle. Not a good sign, I reflected. I sensed protection charms woven into all the protective gear. That was a better sign.

Ironfist raised his right fist over his heart and saluted us before sitting down, "Good morrow on this, the dawn of battle. May your arrows be true and your blades be sharp. If we meet not this night, then I will see you in the halls of the afterlife."

I recognised the Dwarfish battle words. Traditional? Yes. Comforting? No. He sat down and tucked into a bowl of food with gusto.

Madam Mim strode over. The bags under her eyes had grown larger overnight but she was as upright as ever. She asked Aloora and I to follow her. I caught Lorandir's eye but he just shrugged. Aloora was already on her feet so I stretched the kinks out of my shoulders and back and stood up. Mim led us out of the great hall and up another set of spiral stone staircases. We passed more elaborate tapestries and I noticed a theme. All the fae depicted in these scenes were holding scrolls or books or writing. One male scribe was writing with a quill made from an exotic feather that seemed to be bursting into flames. I did a double take when it looked like he'd moved. Madam Mim kept going, unphased by her surroundings and pushed open a large door at the top of the stairs. I took a second to catch my breath, then followed her over the threshold and into a library.

My gnomish friend's eyes lit up as she took in the shelves upon shelves of ancient books and scrolls. Some of them were chained to their ledges. One ancient scroll drifted out of its shelf towards Mim. She caught it deftly and rolled it out on a table in front of the largest stained-glass window I'd ever seen.

The soft morning light shone through the colours in the stained glass making the room seem like it was inside a rainbow. It was oddly calming. I took a deep breath. This was the best I'd felt since arriving in this realm. I stared at the glazed picture of a round table with knights standing around it, holding their weapons and looking like the guardians they were. The protectors of Avalon in life-size stained glass.

A knight in a white and gold tabard had a golden crown depicted over his open-faced helmet. He bore a striking resemblance to the man who had joined us in the sitting room yesterday. I was so slow sometimes. Had we really spoken to King Arthur? I was about to ask Madam Mim when she coughed politely to draw my attention to the scroll now unravelled on the ornate table.

"I wanted to show you this."

I looked down at the picture of a large purple crystal surrounded by tiny black writing that I couldn't understand. Aloora was nodding and smiling and looking at me.

"It's…beautiful?" I tried, unsure of what reaction to go for.

"Does it remind you of anything?"

I fingered my necklace as I tried to rack my brains. It was clearly a large crystal but I hadn't come across anything that large in my jewellery making. I stared at the amethyst around my neck as I thought and then, finally, I made the connection.

"It's an amethyst. Like my necklace," I studied the illustration more closely. The ink had faded over time but it was still a dark purple, a similar colour to the stone hanging around my neck.

"It is exactly like your necklace. I told you once it was a jewel of great value and a powerful protector." I nodded along. That was pretty much what Mim had said when I had been handed the jewel at the shop in Avebury. It had rankled me at the time that the shop attendant had insisted it was a gift and had refused payment but it was a beautiful stone that seemed to protect me from the full brunt of magic attacks. I had lovingly mounted it in copper wire and fashioned the necklace that was now constantly around my neck.

"It is so powerful because it is from Avalon." I blinked at her stupidly. "What I am about to tell you is a closely guarded secret, because in the wrong hands, this knowledge could destroy everything good in the world. The purple amethysts here are the embodiment of the hope and protection that this realm offers everyone – mundane or magic, and this room is the source. I had hoped to invite you here to teach you more, but…another time perhaps."

We were all silent. There were fifty thousand creatures outside Avalon's ward. There might well not be another time. Madam Mim coughed delicately and carried on, "So you are aware that it reacts to magic?"

"It's dampened a few hits that I've taken."

"Exactly," she nodded, "it innately protects you because you hold it. It should also be possible for it to absorb negative energy… such as blood magic."

"Then you should take it!" I struggled to remove it from around my neck.

Mim shook her head, "It is yours. I cannot take it, even if I wanted to. Absorbing energy without it affecting you is difficult and dangerous. It takes much training, but I mention it in case…" she left the sentence unfinished.

"There is one other thing. As the amethyst is from Avalon, it resonates with the other crystals here. They absorb the energy that the people of Avalon generate. Mostly it is positive, but today…"

"So that's why I've been feeling so out of sorts!" I was eager to place the blame for my uncomfortable feelings elsewhere, so I didn't have to think too much about what was to come. It made me feel that I could separate out the despair and the dread, that they weren't my own forebodings but rather those of the fae who lived here.

"Ah, you can feel it. I wondered."

I thought for a moment, "But I don't feel it so much in here…"

"This room is lined with amethysts to protect the magic tomes within. It is here that Avalon will truly stand or fall. If this room is destroyed then it may be too much even if we can rebuild it. But do not trouble yourself with that. I am confident we can prevail. And then I can teach you more about how to control the amethyst you carry."

"If these stones are so powerful, shouldn't we give them to everyone out fighting?"

Mim shook her head, "The stones choose who they go to. I don't fully understand it myself."

"That's fascinating, can I read up on it?" My friend chimed in, reaching her thin fingers towards the scroll. My mouth opened. We were in dire peril and all Aloora wanted to do was study.

Mim nodded with a smile, "Perhaps another time."

Aloora had the good grace to look a little embarrassed. Madam Mim led us back to the great hall. I heard her skirts rustle along the floor as I stroked the jewel around my neck absently. An amethyst of Avalon. And I was wearing it like an everyday piece of jewellery. I must have still been looking bemused when we entered the hall because Lorandir stood and asked if I was alright. I nodded dazedly.

He had found some armour in my absence and was looking every inch the elven prince in a moulded breastplate made of the same lacquered material as the Morthimas's armour. It had an antiquated look to it. I traced the intricate patterns on his armguards and greaves with my eyes and hoped it was serviceable armour, not just the fancy decorative stuff you sometimes saw on display in museums. He put his arm around my shoulders as we walked outside.

Chapter 17

In the morning light, the small homesteads looked quaint and the sort of fairy tale cottages I could imagine in mainland Europe, perhaps halfway up an alpine mountain. Now they were surrounded by armoured magical beings. The air buzzed with magical auras and spells. I briefly wondered where the refugees and children were from last night before a squalling baby sounded from inside the castle. Of course. That would be the safest place for everyone who wasn't fighting. My stomach twisted nervously and I gripped Lorandir's hand for comfort. He felt cool against my sweaty palms.

Madam Mim led us up some white stone steps to the top of the gate. I gazed up at the ward shimmering above us. In the daylight it glowed a shade between lavender and violet. I narrowed my eyes. I had thought it was a hemispherical dome, but now I could see that it was more complex than that. Sort of a dodecahedron or whatever a two-hundred-sided shape was called. And at each corner, an amethyst like the one around my neck twinkled in the morning sunshine. I frowned. One crystal, the one closest to where the enemy was massed, was a darker colour than the others.

I turned my gaze and looked out over the troops lined up neatly, careful not to look directly down from our platform. I risked slipping on my newly acquired sunglasses and was instantly dazzled by the many colours. It looked like a rainbow on acid. There was a swathe of bright pink that denoted the fae folk. The elves were forest green and the dwarves were red, a darker shade than my own pale red aura. Beyond the ward, muted by the shield spell, I could see a jumble of darker colours; slimy green goblins, orange orc auras and blue troll ones.

There were unfamiliar auras too; rusty red the shade of dried blood and one that blazed as bright as fire. I pulled off the sunglasses and rubbed my eyes. As I focused without the tinted lenses, I could see the forces more clearly. There were the golden feathered and fur coats of the gryphons amongst the shining elven troops. Another troop of elves was on horseback. I looked again. No, they were riding unicorns. The fantastical creatures looked bloodthirsty as they pawed the ground. I noted the elves were all riding bareback.

The fae were lined up next to them but managed to be completely separate from the more orderly elves. They had brightly coloured hair against shiny metallic skin of every shade from bronze to blue steel. I fingered the anti-glamour charm Gunther, my father's friend and my supplier, had given me.

Without their glamour, the fae had pointed noses and eyes that were slightly too large for their faces, reminding me of glittering insects. Their armour consisted of animal hides with the fur still attached. I thought I recognised the large irregular black spots of a cow hide and something that might once have been a tiger but I couldn't place a shaggy blue-black hide that several of them were wearing.

Some of them sported wings, folded against their backs and glinting with iridescent colours as they caught the sunlight. I squinted as I tried to get a view of their mounts. It looked like some of them were riding giant snails. The shells were painted with swirling Celtic designs. I wanted to ask someone how effective a snail could be in battle but then the tall man in the white and gold tabard stepped forward and whispered something in Madam Mim's ear. He pointed towards the shield barrier. A single figure was standing next to it, just below the darker gem connecting the corner of the ward, hands behind its back, waiting.

Madam Mim sighed and strode down the steps. We all followed. She gave a low whistle and her corgis ran to meet her. She harnessed them to a Celtic style chariot that was parked against a wall. I stared at the sight of the two stumpy legged dogs strapped to a war chariot. The darker corgi's tongue was lolling from its mouth. Then they began to transform.

The cute, fluffy creatures disappeared and were replaced by larger, more dangerous canines. Their eyes flared an amber colour and their bodies grew and morphed until they were the size of small horses. I stepped back from their newly lengthened teeth as they gnashed their jaws. Smoke began to rise from the dogs as they assumed their true forms. Now I understood how these were mounts. She told us all to stay where we were before speaking a command to the wish hounds. They sprung forward and Madam Mim raced towards the figure, manoeuvring her chariot past the massed troops with ease.

Agent Jones clearly wasn't happy. She folded her arms and tapped her foot on the cobble stone floor of the courtyard. "Dzrak it! I wish there was some way we could know what's going on."

"I might be able to help…" a middle aged witch sporting a long, blonde ponytail stepped forward, carrying an electronic tablet with a large screen. I recognised her as one of the Omensford coven. She waved her hand over the tablet and Mim appeared as if we were streaming a film. The sorceress' face was grim as she raced to meet the single figure.

"Fascinating!" Maxi dragged his hand through his white hair, making it stand on end in a mad professor style. He bent forward to get a closer look, "Scrying through technology, yah?"

Agent Jones grabbed her colleague firmly by the shoulder and pulled him back so he wasn't blocking the screen. He opened his mouth as if to reply before catching himself and saving it for later. By the way he was rocking on his heels, I guessed he was desperate to find out how the scrying tablet worked.

Madam Mim had reached the barrier and stepped down from her chariot. She stood directly in front of the dark figure and motioned to the ward. The triangular side of the polyhedronical ward between them became clear so they could see each other. The male figure standing opposite her had grey skin and pointed ears. I heard an intake of breath from behind me.

"Dark elf!"

I studied him more closely. He looked a little more muscled than the lean elves I had seen in Breconia and his eyes were sharp and cruel. But there was something familiar about him. He was dressed in black leather armour, trimmed with decorative sliver-coloured buckles. A serrated sword hung at his hip. If it wasn't for his piercing eyes and commanding stance, he wouldn't have looked out of place at a sci-fi convention.

"I am Morgan le Fay, custodian of Avalon," Madam Mim's voice sounded powerful but far away through the screen. I had to stop myself from elbowing Aloora at the revelation that the tall sorceress was a living legend. Mim continued, "I treat on behalf of all hope and light and love protected herein. Who has come to my domain?"

"Do you not recognise me? I am Mordred, son of Arthur Pendragon. I speak on behalf of all gathered here," he gestured to the army at his back.

I gasped at the revelation and looked again. His eyes looked wilder and his hair was styled differently but it was the same dark elf I'd met at the coronation. I heard a groan behind me and then the man in the white and gold tabard pushed to the front. Definitely King Arthur then. He seemed about to grab the tablet when a hand stopped him. Arthur looked down at the age-spotted skin and then up into the face of Merlin. The old sorcerer shook his head sadly and pulled Arthur back to watch.

"Why are you here?" Mim asked. One arched eyebrow was all the surprise she showed at Arthur's son leading an army to her gate.

"For the same reason all come to Avalon. We seek aid and shelter."

"You have a funny way of seeking it when you are all armed and have been attacking my shields all night."

"We only carry what we need to defend ourselves and we have been seeking a way in to present our petition."

"I will hear it now."

"We are those who are pursued and hated. We were driven from our homes, hunted by those who call us monsters. We want peace."

I looked up at the massed horde gathered outside the magical barrier. Funny way to seek peace by bringing an army to Avalon's doorstep. A roar sounded from the horde. They sure sounded like monsters to me.

"If peace is what you wish for, you can have it. We have no wish to fight," Madam Mim sounded cautious but hopeful.

Mordred inclined his head slightly before pulling back and meeting Mim's sharp black eyes, "And we ask for a realm to live in."

Madam Mim let out a long-suffering sigh, "You have a realm, Mordred. Be at peace there."

"A realm?! You sent me into exile in a twisted land of darkness. It is the worst of places. We could not survive there. When we tried to come back into the world, we were turned upon. My people have been hunted out of existence and you call that mercy? We are barely tolerated and we are feared by those who once called us kin." Flecks of spittle flew from his pale lips as he listed the wrongs he had been done.

I thought of the elves who had turned away from his retinue of dark elves at the coronation. I felt a pang of sympathy for someone not accepted by others. It was how I'd felt in Breconia too. But I'd been there for love, not to distract the elves in the hope they wouldn't defend Avalon, because it was suddenly clear to me what had been going on when I'd interrupted Mordred and the councillor that night. They had been plotting to prevent Morthimas from entering the battle. I tuned back in to the conversation playing out on the small screen.

"The land you were sent to was once a beautiful place. It has been twisted by your own soul and the hatred you have taught your people; it is a reflection of you. When you left it, your people sought to spread discord throughout the known universe. They made enemies with all and were then surprised to be attacked."

"Not enemies with all…no, in my exile, I have found some allies. Do you not see them here today, ready to support me and claim our place?" he smirked as the crowd behind him let out a roar of approval. "We are those who have been shunned and hated and yet we deserve a place to live and work and raise our families. We only ask for a place to call our own."

"And I'm sure you have another realm in mind?"

"Oh yes," the dark elf smiled nastily, "Avalon will do quite nicely."

"You know what you are asking is impossible."

"Then we will take it!"

"While there is breath in my body, I will not let you take this realm," Madam Mim turned to head back to her chariot, her long skirts swishing against the lush grass and meadow flowers.

"Then you will have to die!" Mordred leapt forward, drawing his sword and lunging towards her. It glowed a rusty red as he funnelled magic into the blade. The magical shield surrounding Avalon flickered. Mim looked over her shoulder and with a shrug, the barrier intensified. Mordred shrieked in fury as he tried to push through the ward. It held.

Mim made a gesture over her throat and then began to speak. Her voice was amplified and it echoed across the massed troops. They turned to her with rapt attention, wanting inspiration.

"Thank you, friends of Avalon, for joining me in this, our darkest hour. The day ahead may be hard but we fight with love and hope on our side. There is no one I'd rather be with. Trust your commanders and trust yourselves."

There was a pause as the army lay waiting for more. King Arthur stepped forward, out of the courtyard and faced Avalon's forces. He glowed visibly with golden threads of magic. He pulled his long sword from its jewelled scabbard and raised it aloft. It managed to catch the morning sunlight in a blaze of light. My eyes widened. If that was Arthur, then his blade was Excalibur.

"For Avalon and for glory!"

The massed army repeated his cry. To my shame, I found myself thinking that if we survived, I'd have to ask Arthur if

I could hold the famous sword, just once. Then I pushed the thought from my mind. We had to get through today first. The commanders must have given some sort of order because, as one, the army wheeled round and began to march toward the ward where Mordred was now concentrating his magical attacks, joined by enchanters from his army.

The control of the Avalonian troops was incredible. They marched in silence, the sunlight glittering as it caught the metallic helmets and breastplates. It really did look like a golden army of hope. The front section split into two and I noticed the elven unicorn riders disappeared as they moved away from the castle. Invisibility spell. I frowned. It had looked like they were heading in a different direction to the rest of the army. I wanted to ask someone about it but Lorandir and Morthimas were having an argument behind me.

"You can't fight!"

"I'm the king and I intend to lead my troops into battle. Besides, it's not like you have any experience fighting dark elves!"

"I'm a better shot than you!"

"I want you to stay here…in case something happens. You would be my choice as heir."

"I cannot be your heir and you know it." Lorandir folded his arms defiantly.

"Cousin…"

"If you stay here in the castle, you won't need to choose an heir!"

King Morthimas shook his head stubbornly.

"Then so be it, cousin, we will fight together."

They fell into a hug before pulling apart, embarrassed at the display of emotion.

"Ahem, ahem," Maxi interrupted the moment with a fake cough, "I brought these communicators for us. Modified so we can use them even with the magical distortion what!" He handed out the small radio-like devices and gave a few extra to Arthur and the elven king to hand out to the commanders. He spoke quickly as he explained how to use them.

King Arthur looked genuinely amazed that one press of a button meant he could talk to someone across the battlefield. He surreptitiously attempted to try it out but the whine of feedback from being too close to other devices shrieked loudly, causing the king to cover his ears in shock. Maxi took the device from him and turned it off, instantly cutting out the horrible noise.

"Best to use them when you're in position, yah?"

King Arthur nodded regally and walked away cradling the radios he'd been given. Agent Jones signalled to Aloora and I.

"Right, I don't want you two in the fray," we started to protest, but it was half-hearted. What could we do to help? "You're best used on those towers. Look out over the battle and radio in when you see any significant enemy movements. It would be better if we had a drone, but we lost that…" she spared a glance at Aloora who looked at her shoes guiltily, "so you're our best chance. Get some protective gear on and get us some intel!"

She rummaged in her fake crocodile skin handbag and pulled out a pair of binoculars and what looked like a sniper scope. She thrust them at us before turning to the next Magical Liaison Office agent.

"Maxi – I want you working on our portals and interdimensional comms. I want more MLO officers here ASAP and we need an escape route if things go south. See if you can use the crystals to help bolster the signal somehow." I could tell the situation was bleak, because she'd slipped into using acronyms. Maxi started to protest that it didn't work like that, but Agent Jones carried on, pointing at Marco who had followed us up the stairs, "You. You're not supposed to be here but make yourself useful and help Maxi. Take one of the witches with you, she might be able to help if you need any magic."

"I'll go," the same middle-aged woman who had scryed for us stepped forward, "I have an affinity for electronics." There was a snort from one of the other witches and the woman clarified, "Well…about fifty per cent of the time, the rest of the time it's less affinity and more blow up…" She flicked her long ponytail and sparks flew from her fingers. Her hair frizzed a little at the electric current she gave off. I had no trouble believing she was a tech witch with those flashes. She sauntered off after Maxi and Marco. I heard her introducing herself as Fi as they went.

A sharp whistle sounded near my ear. I turned to see two large gryphons approaching us. The golden animals swooped down and landed on the white stones, their lion's feet landing softly on the stone. I recognised Finn, Lorandir's gryphon and reached up to stroke his feathery head. He clacked his beak at me.

“Sorry, no treats today Finn,” Errol started squirming on my shoulder, annoyed by the larger predators. I patted him absentmindedly and put him on the ground so he was further from their fierce beaks. From the corner of my eye, I saw Aloora approach Morthimas’ gryphon. She loved the large creatures and I knew she was excited to be near them again. She’d be out there riding with them if Agent Jones hadn’t ordered us to watch from the towers. I turned my attention back to the elf next to me. So this was it. Lorandir really was going to fight. I turned to him and blinked back tears. “Take care out there and don’t die, OK.”

He swept me into a warm embrace. I felt my face heat with automatic embarrassment at a public display of affection, but I returned his kiss fiercely. He tucked a loose strand of hair behind my ear and whispered, “I love you galad’Amethysta and I will see you again.”

I wanted to give him a talisman to keep him safe. I started to remove my necklace with its powers of protection, but he put his hand over mine preventing me. I choked a little then moved my free hand over his armour. I traced every Dwarfish rune of protection I could think of, willing my magic into the metal worked over the lacquered surface of his armour. I felt the amethyst heat as I continued and I hoped it was lending me some of its power. It would take a miracle for all of us to survive the horde massed outside the ward. Then he was stepping away from me and mounting his gryphon. He bent down to give me another kiss then spurred his mount into the air.

"I love you too," I whispered. I picked up Errol and held the small wyrm tightly as I felt a fat tear run down my cheek.

Agent Jones and Dot strode forwards, both touting swords and crossbows. Their supernatural speed allowed them to reach Madam Mim and her chariot in record time. Espretha followed behind. I saw her hesitate as she passed the ranks of elves, but they must have sensed her warped magic, damaged from her time in the cult. Those closest to her turned their backs, their armour clacking with the sound of lacquered wood on wood as they moved. I saw her lips form a scowl before she held her head high and jogged after Agent Jones and Dot.

Aloora and I raced to our vantage point at the top of the tallest tower. Both out of breath, I watched Mordred attack the same amethyst suspended in the ward's spell over and over. I saw it darken from purple to grey to black as the evil army blasted it again and again. I heard Aloora speak into the radio a split second before the jewel flickered and shattered into thousands of shards. One part of the shield had failed. The fight had begun.

Chapter 18

The Avalonian army waited. The plan seemed to be to funnel the enemy army through the small opening in the shield and deal with them quickly so their numbers couldn't count for much. Initially it seemed to work. The first wave of goblins with their ramshackle armour poured through and were cut down by volleys of arrows from the elves and fae waiting inside the ward.

I had read about battles in books and seen recreations in films, but the reality was nothing like either of those. Gore, blood and guts spilled from the small goblins as they were mown down. They lay on the floor. I imagined I could hear their groans over the roars of both sides as they worked themselves into a battle frenzy. One small goblin tried to crawl away and was hit by another arrow as he pulled himself pitifully across the grass. I tore the spyglass away from my face to avoid seeing the casualties.

Aloora was pale next to me but she kept her binoculars firmly to her eyes.

"Are you alright?" I put my hand on her shoulder.

"No. This is awful."

"Look away then Ally."

My friend shook her head, "We've got a job to do. Avalon is more important than my feelings about battle."

Suitably chastened, I took a deep breath and held the sniper's scope back to my eye. "Is it my imagination or is the gap getting wider?"

I scanned the ward and soon saw enemy warlocks or witches bombarding the magical barrier with cruel looking spells. Thy were focusing their attacks with deadly precision on the crystals next to the gap in the ward. Despite Mim and Merlin's awesome power and control, the enemy was indeed forcing the break in the barrier wider. The amethysts were shattering one by one.

"Wargs!"

Aloora's cry drew my attention away from the magical attack. Huge hideous dog-like creatures were zipping through the enemy forces and towards the opening. I pressed the button on our communicator and shouted into it.

Agent Jones' voice crackled back, "We need more specifics. How many? Where? Over."

"A dzraktun of wargs heading your way, towards the opening! Now!"

I didn't hear Agent Jones reply and switched back to watching the battle. The wargs had made it through the gap in the barrier and were tearing towards the archers. I wanted to close my eyes but the horror drew me back. Through the telescopic lens, the creatures looked more like hyenas than dogs and their oversized teeth were prominent as they opened their jaws wide, ready for the kill.

A horn sounded a long note and there was a loud cry from the fae. The snail riders rushed forward. The gigantic snails were much faster than the ones that plagued Mum's garden and I watched as they flattened the wargs. Once the snails had ripped through the main band of wargs, all that was left was twitching corpses coated with slime. One snail stopped, its gaping mouth opened, and it devoured one of the stray wargs in a strange undulating motion. I wanted to throw up as it sucked the struggling warg into its innards.

Two wargs outside of the direct hit threw themselves at the nearest gastropod. They bounced off its shell, smearing the blue war markings without leaving a dent in the shell. They tried again and this time aimed for the head. The snail's eyes bulged as it saw them coming. In an instant, it was inside its shell, leaving the wargs whining as they sailed into thin air. The fae rider atop the shell finished them off with a couple of accurate arrows.

The snails plunged on through the gap and cut thick swathes into the enemy troops. Many of the goblins turned to flee and were crushed as those behind clamoured forward. One snail was downed after three ogres pushed it onto its side. Its vulnerable opening exposed, long spears soon finished it up. It bubbled out slime long after it was dead.

The fae on the ground used the slime trails to propel themselves forward like expert figure skaters and they were soon out in the midst of the horde. The battlefield exploded with coloured magic and enchanted weapons as they moved forward. They were less an organised troop and more a band of warriors fighting for glory as they pushed on. I watched with horror as one of them stopped to saw off the head of a fallen enemy captain – a large orc complete with tusks and a long black feather sticking out of its helmet.

"Tell the fae to stop collecting heads and keep fighting!" I screamed into the communicator. The fae commander must have had one of the radios as I saw her glance backwards before aiming a small spell at the offending head-chopper. He glared at her and raised his weapon before jumping back into the fray.

I looked up from the fae and tried to find my friends. It was impossible. I had no idea where they were in the confusion of the fight and I scanned our troops in vain for confirmation that Lorandir or Dot or Agent Jones were still alive.

I caught sight of Mim's war chariot cutting a path through the battle. Her wish hounds were mauling anyone foolish enough to get in her way. As I watched her progress, I saw long blades zing from her chariot wheels. She curved her chariot in a wide arc, cutting down enemies left and right as she went.

A blur of movement and a whirl of a long, blonde plait near her side told me Espretha was fighting with her. She was using the chariot as a platform for acrobatics as she leapt off, swiped with her long daggers and then retreated to the protection of the vehicle. It was an effective strategy. I zoomed my spyglass in on her blood-spattered face before more cries drew my attention away.

I swept the battlefield with my spyglass and then felt a surge of magic. I tried to pinpoint the source and saw Merlin, hanging back from the fight. He was standing to one side, muttering as he whirled his staff so fast it nearly knocked off his pointed hat. He looked like an archetypal wizard, straight out of Lord of the Rings. I blinked as I had the thought that he probably was the archetypal wizard.

His staff stopped twirling and a huge bolt of lightning crackled from the sky. I scanned the horde. In the middle of the enemy lines, a large scorch mark had appeared with one of the giants standing in the middle of the burning grass. It swayed for a couple of seconds before raising the tree it was holding as a club. Then it toppled backwards, crushing some hapless dark elves under its huge body. I jerked the spyglass back to Merlin. He was now leaning on his staff, swaying slightly at the power he had expended. As I watched, he staggered to the shelter of a nearby tree and sat down, his hat nodding over his face. If I didn't know better, I'd have said he'd gone to sleep.

Aloora grabbed the radio from me, "Giant!"

I opened my mouth to tell her that Merlin had just killed it when I clocked the other massive humanoid striding down the rightmost side of the battlefield. He was going to swoop around the horde and get to the gap in the ward, where our troops were still pouring out.

I shouted and tried to point but that was stupid. Aloora had a more precise approach as she frowned at the giant and spoke into the communicator, "Heading South. Less than two minutes."

Out of nowhere, the unicorn riders appeared to the right and bore down on the enemy.

“Unicorns!” I pointed and Aloora swung her binoculars to the newly appeared riders.

“Scots elves,” she muttered under her breath before relaying the message through the radio.

The unicorns were ferocious, their heads lowered as they prepared for impact. Through the sniper scope, I could see the sweat on their flanks and the spittle flying from their mouths. Their eyes glowed gold and silver as they charged. The elf riders loosed off volley after volley of arrows until they were too close.

Undeterred, they drew their curved swords and cut down anyone in their way as they fought towards the giant. The cries sounded loud. The giant turned and roared. It raised its club and swung it, knocking five unicorns down. Their riders jumped free and turned, blades swinging as they fought valiantly. The giant’s return swing took out more elves as the unicorns tried to halt their charge. An elf rider stood on their unicorn’s back and aimed an arrow at the giant’s head. It bellowed in pain and gripped its eye with a hand. I saw blood trickle from beneath its fingers.

Blind in one eye, the giant lashed out wildly, crushing elves, unicorns and its own troops underfoot. Another elf balanced atop a unicorn and launched itself up at the giant’s head, sword out, aiming to cut its throat. But the giant was moving and caught the elf with a fat hand. The elf struggled as the giant squeezed. I fancied I could hear the crack of bones as the elf was crushed and the giant dropped its lifeless corpse onto the ground.

A large clearing had formed around the giant as no one wanted to be trampled. An elf wielding two swords got behind the massive creature and slit its hamstrings with sharp blades. The giant toppled forwards onto its knees. It was far from helpless and continued to assault anyone it could reach, not caring if they were friend or foe.

Several unicorns were still alive and bent their heads to charge at the sides of the giant while it swatted at two elves attacking its other side. It roared again as the unicorns' horns came away bloody. One had a string of gut looped around its dark horn. I swallowed the vomit that burned the back of my throat. The same elf that had brought the giant to its knees now climbed up its back, using the giant's own tree-bark armour for handholds. The giant must have felt something as it reached to claw fruitlessly at its own back. The elf was too agile and continued its climb. Once at the giant's shoulders, the elf plunged its swords into the huge neck, severing its spine. Then the elf had pulled out their swords, back flipped off the giant as it tumbled to the ground and continued to fight.

The battlefield was chaos but I began to think we might win. Both giants were down. The snails had cut a large path into the horde and the unicorns were still stampeding.

The morning sunlight faded behind gathering clouds that darkened the sky. The clouds thickened and turned a deep grey until they obscured the aurora colours of the fae sky completely. The sudden darkness made it harder to see the battlefield. It appeared as one mass of fighting, harder than ever to tell friend from foe. I shivered suddenly. Errol pricked his claws into my neck as he moved nervously. A storm was coming. Something wasn't right.

Then I heard a gut-wrenching roar and a shadow swept over us.

Chapter 19

Aloora and I stared in horror as a dragon passed over the dark forces. It let out another evil roar and then a blast of lightning shot from its throat across the Avalonian forces. I heard my friend's gasp.

"I didn't think it was possible…"

That was reassuring. Not. I heard her speak into her communicator, warning the commanders about the new threat. The soldiers had noticed the dragon and a group of archers were loosing arrows too fast for me to follow. They bounced off the dragon's thick hide. After another couple of passes, the dragon turned towards the castle itself.

A band of gryphon-riders made to intercept it. I couldn't tear my eyes away as the huge dragon twisted and grabbed one of them mid-air with its terrible talons. The rider lost their grip and fell to the ground a second before the injured gryphon plummeted.

I shouted Lorandir's name but I had no idea if he was among the riders. The pack of gryphons changed tactics and moved away from the dragon. Instead the riders harried it with arrows and blasts of magic. The dragon shrieked in annoyance. I saw a pulse of red magic spread out from the dragon's neck. Aloora was frowning.

"Dragons can't use magic like that…"

Then we saw the rider. A small figure all in black was seated on the dragon's back. Aloora put her hands to her mouth.

"Impossible! There hasn't been a dragon rider in millennia!"

"Well there is now. What do we do?"

She shook her head then swore, sounding like a cross between a hissing cat and a bag of gravel being dropped. I stared at my friend. She could speak several languages fluently and that was the worst swearing I had ever heard from her.

"He asked me about commands in Draconic. I told him everything," Aloora's hands started to shake. I reached out to comfort her and realised that she was shaking with anger. Mordred had used her.

Another roar pulled us back to the battle. The dragon twisted around in a circle and added its own lightning breath to the pulse of magic. The gryphons all fell from the sky. Every single one. I screamed. I ran to the edge of the wall and leaned over. I wanted a glimpse of Lorandir. I had to know he was alright. I overbalanced.

The ground loomed before me. Time felt suspended as I hung over the sheer drop. Errol scrabbled frantically, digging his sharp claws into my flesh. Aloora grabbed my arm and jerked me backwards. I shot her a smile of thanks then returned to the wall, hanging onto a crenulation.

Just before the gryphons hit the ground, they slowed. I scanned the castle walls and saw one of the Omensford witches muttering with her hands out. I sent her a silent thank you, watching her through my spyglass.

Her face creased with pain. A stray arrow had struck her in the leg and she collapsed, clutching her thigh. The elves and their gryphons thudded to the ground and were swarmed by orcs. Someone screamed. It took a few seconds for me to realise the sound was coming from my mouth. I sank to my knees and sent a prayer to whatever god was listening to save Lorandir and the others.

Aloora pulled me upright, her eyes filled with sympathy. "We still have a job to do," she murmured as she wrapped her arms around me. I nodded and wiped my eyes, pushing back the tears. There wasn't time to weep now. I put the sniper scope back to my eye and tried to focus but when I looked back to the battlefield, the dragon had disappeared behind the storm clouds.

I searched the field. Nothing. Schiztz. How can we lose a dragon?

I spotted the flaming ifrit circling behind the horde. The fire demon looked like it was moving purposefully. I frowned as I tried to puzzle out where it was going. Then I saw the group of dryads and living trees near the forest. If those caught fire, the whole forest could go up in flames. I snatched the communicator from Aloora's hand and radioed everyone.

"Ifrit. Heading for the forest."

Aloora and I leant over the ramparts as we watched the fire demon move closer. Then there was a roar somewhere between a bonfire and a jet engine above the sounds of battle. It had been hit. I strained to see what was happening. The ifrit had stopped moving forwards and was instead swatting the ground around it. Occasionally a shot of blue would appear on its fiery form.

The demon raised its arms, gathering its power and exploded in a fiery supernova. The flames set light to nearby dark elves who didn't have any fire charms protecting them. They fled from the ifrit, trying to put themselves out. The blue-ish spots continued to appear on the demon's form. I saw a figure dancing around before it jumped out of the way of a fireball and disappeared.

"It's Dot!" shouted Aloora, adjusting her binoculars. The vampire used her speed to keep the fire demon occupied with the ice sword I had enchanted. But even vampiric speed couldn't keep her safe. The demon swept its arms wide and a circle of fire appeared around it. Dot rolled but the flames caught her arm and spread down her clothing. I watched in horror as the left side of her body turned black. She staggered to one side, narrowly dodging a fireball. Through the telescopic lens, I could see her gritted teeth as she clutched her icy sword.

Aloora nudged me and pointed. I shirted my gaze. A lone figure had approached to help. More clouds appeared above them, lower than the ones already in the sky and a deluge of rain poured directly onto the ifrit. Steam burst from it as the water evaporated on contact. I heard its roar as it turned around. It couldn't see. Dot used the opportunity to leap in and aim a blow at its head. Another roar blasted through my ears. Merlin joined the weather witch. His tall hat recognisable even from here. I wondered how he had got there so fast from his sleeping spot and whether he had any power left.

I needn't have worried. He poured his power into the stormy clouds and the temperature dropped. I shivered even atop the tower as the rain turned to hail. I fancied I could hear the sizzle as it hit the ifrit's fiery form. The demon was on its knees. It swiped at Dot. She somersaulted over its large hand and sunk the sword between its eyes. I saw her face tighten in pain as her feet connected with its fiery form.

She held on, even as her skin charred. It keeled to one side and the living flame went dark. Ice spread over it and Dot kept the sword in for an instant longer to be sure it was dead before falling to the ground in a heap. Her blackened body lay still. I felt a tear make its way down my cheek as a cheer sounded from the army of Avalon and they pressed the attack.

A downdraught caused me and Aloora to duck. Errol hissed angrily. Aloora squinted upwards, "The dragon!"

We watched helplessly as it landed in the courtyard. It let out an awful sound that had me covering my ears. Mordred was seated atop it. He jumped down lightly and smiled. Long spurs on the heels of his shoes sparked off the cobblestones. I could see his smug look of satisfaction through the sniper scope. We both ducked behind the white stone wall as he turned in our direction. Schiztz. What were we going to do now?

"Look! It's been captured, the poor thing."

I turned to see my friend pointing at the courtyard. She was talking about the dragon of all things. I stared at my friend. Sometimes her priorities were out of alignment. With a shake of my head, I put the sniper scope back to my eye and peered past the pristine stone to look at the dragon more closely. There was a saddle fastened to its neck but under that, golden blood trickled down its sapphire blue scales.

Schiztz. Maybe it really had been captured. But how much magic could Mordred have that he was able to subdue a dragon? I moved the scope around. He was walking towards the great hall. Where everyone who couldn't fight was sheltering. And where Marco and Maxi were. Schiztz. I turned back to Aloora but she had gone. Dzrak it all. I grabbed the radio and garbled out something about the dragon and Mordred. Then I ran.

Chapter 20

I flew down the stone steps and tried a door at random. It opened easily. I headed in the direction I thought the Great Hall was in and kept running. I sent a silent prayer of thanks to Espretha for her forced training. The runs around Bute Park were really paying off. I kept going and ended up back on another section of the ramparts running around the castle of Avalon. I caught a glimpse of Aloora approaching the dragon. I shouted out to her. And succeeded in getting the dragon to switch its attention to me. It gathered lightning in its throat and unleashed it.

I dove to one side and plummeted through another door and back into the relative safety of the castle. Behind me, the crackle of lightning cascaded against the stone. I ploughed on, choosing a set of stairs that led down towards the ground floor. At the bottom, I stopped and tried to think as I caught my breath. Mordred was probably already inside the great hall so the only thing going for me was surprise. I edged my way as quietly as I could to the heavy wooden door. It was open. Inside was in shadow so I couldn't see anything. I reached into my belt where I had hooked the radio. It was gone.

Schiztz. I was on my own. I released Bane from its holster, took a breath and stepped up to the threshold.

I stepped through and blinked as my eyes adjusted to the shady interior. Maxi was on the floor, his hair stuck up in all directions. The tech witch, Fi, was standing over him protectively. She turned as she heard my heavy boots on the floor, her hands sparking wildly and her long hair frizzed into crinkly static wisps. Mordred was in front of her, his sword raised.

"No!" I shouted and ran to them. The witch let off a shower of sparks at the dark elf. He cried out and reached to protect his eyes. There was a strange static sensation coming from the witch. It was almost painful, like putting a battery on your tongue. I winced and muttered the Dwarfish word to activate the shield on my axe. Mordred cursed and struck with his serrated sword. It bounced off my magic.

"Fools!" yelled the dark elf, "I don't have time for your games!"

He waved his hands above his head and off-red magic swirled in the air. It seeped into the vaulted beams, twisting around them insidiously. I heard the crack of wood. With a nasty grin, Mordred strode out of the room. I flung myself over Maxi and the witch, the battery-like feeling of her magic intensified as I touched her. Errol let out a terrified roar in my ear and I willed the shield to hold as the roof came down on us.

After the splintering and crashing had stopped, I opened my eyes. We were surrounded by rubble but unhurt. The magic from my axe had created a small hollow for us. I let out the breath I was holding and released the shield. A stray beam as thick as my waist slid to one side, crashing to the floor and raising more dust.

"Maxi?" I asked, "Did Mordred hurt you?"

He groaned slightly.

"Actually, that was me. I might have given the portal too much of a boost and given him a small electric shock…" Fi twirled a strand of her hair guiltily, trying to smooth her frizzy hair back into place.

Maxi came round, his hair standing on end like he was holding a balloon charged with static electricity. He blinked up at us, "Oh, hi Amethyst, you're here are you? Battle over then, yah?" He coughed and rubbed a dark spot on his wrist where Fi's power had scorched his skin.

"Er not exactly over…where's Marco? And everyone else? Weren't people hiding in here?"

"Got the portal open and everyone through to the Office."

That was good news.

"We were just waiting for the Magical Liaison Office agents to come through and support here when Mordred showed up," Fi added.

"Mordred was here?" Maxi's eyes goggled. Then he looked round, taking in the debris that surrounded us. He blinked, "We've got to stop him!" Maxi stood, then sat back down hard as his left leg twitched violently.

"Sorry," grimaced Fi, "there might be some muscle spasms. Side effect of too much electricity."

“There isn’t time for this!” Maxi’s voice was getting higher as he started to panic. I rubbed my forehead, trying to think.

“OK, radio Agent Jones and the others, let them know what’s happened then get the portal open and get more agents here.”

“What are you going to do?”

“Madam Mim showed me the source of Avalon’s power. Hopefully Mordred doesn’t know where it is. I’ll go there.”

“He’ll kill you!”

“Thanks for the vote of confidence! But I’ll be fine, don’t even worry about it…” I paused, “but the sooner you can get back-up here the better.”

That said, I hauled myself up onto the large blocks of roof that had caved into the great hall and made my way to the corridor that led to the library.

Chapter 21

I tried to reach out with my magic as I ran along the stone corridor. I cursed softly and slipped the enchanted sunglasses on in case I could make out Mordred's aura. No luck. My affinity was always with metal rather than stone. Desperate, I held out my hand and let my fingers run along the wall as I ran, trying to sense anything that might tell me where Mordred was or if I was too late. The amethyst around my neck warmed under my clothing and I hoped it was boosting my powers.

I felt the walls of Avalon stretching above and below me and a strange song sounded in my head without going through my ears. I felt compelled to follow it. The crystals were leading me to the library. I sped up. Back in the other direction, I could feel something out of place. Connected to the fabric of the castle, I could sense Avalon's displeasure. The crystals were reacting to something. Mordred's magic I guessed. That was good. He wasn't heading to the library. There was still a chance.

I got to the gilded wooden doors of the library and rushed in. I pressed my hand to the metal hinges and willed them to be quiet before pushing the doors shut. They were well oiled and glided under my touch. Safely inside, I used my enchanted key that could fit any lock to secure the door, grateful for dwarven ingenuity. Then I enchanted the metallic mechanism so only I could open it. I felt my magic curl around the complex locking mechanism and hoped it would hold. I turned and tried to think. What would Agent Jones do?

"She'd prob'ly make some sort of barricade."

I jumped at the unexpected voice behind me and Errol let off a small burst of nervous flames. I hadn't realised I'd spoken that last thought aloud and I certainly hadn't expected an answer. I turned quickly, my hand resting on my axe ready to pull it from its holds. Gary the gargoyle sat perched on the large fireplace. Through the tinted lenses, his aura shone a mossy stone colour. That seemed appropriate for a gargoyle. He gave me a twisted smile and a thumbs up.

I clutched my chest theatrically, "You nearly gave me a heart attack!"

His grin grew wider then he spoke, "I didn't know I affected 'oo so much! Well wot are 'oo waiting for? Oo can't be staring in my soulful eyes all day, oo've gotta barricade to build."

Create a barricade. Right. I grabbed chairs and piled them against the door. I considered the books on their shelves with their strangely ethereal auras. Most of them were varying shades of purple through the tinted lenses of the sunglasses. A few were the forest green of elves and there were a couple of dark red dwarven auras too. A whole shelf of them gave off an ominous black aura, sucking the colour from the room. I noticed thick chains binding those books shut. I shuddered and considered whether they might stop Mordred or hurt me if I moved them.

In the end, I left all of them on their shelves, feeling it might be some sort of sacrilege to use magical tomes to try to keep the door shut, even if some of them were almost the same height as me. Instead I moved to the enormous table. With a sigh and then a grunt of effort, I managed to lift one end.

"You could help you know!"

Gary watched me lug the heavy table across the room. He shrugged, "Nah, I'm too small for lifting fings like that."

I kept going, moving the table by inches to the door. When I was done, I leaned against it, panting. Gary stared at me in silence. When I had got my breath back, I unharnessed my ancestral axe and stood in a fighting pose facing the door. I tried not to think about the battle still raging outside.

Or my friends who were in it. Or Lorandir who was probably dead or injured when his gryphon fell from the sky. Or Dot who had burned to a crisp killing the ifrit. Or the evil sorcerer who was trying to destroy Avalon and would likely kill me on the way. I choked a little and blinked back the hot tears that threatened to fall. To distract myself, I started walking, still holding Bane, ready to fight. I had made my choice. This was my last stand.

"So, it's just 'oo and me, hey?" the gargoyle said suggestively with a lewd wink.

I clutched Bane more tightly. I was nervous and didn't feel like playing Gary's games now I'd decided I'd fight or fall here. Probably fall. I kept one eye on the door as I paced in front of the fireplace where Gary was perched.

"Aren't you worried?"

"Well," the small gargoyle scratched his pointed ear with one hand, "the way I see it, the worst has already happened to me."

I turned, curious, "So what did happen to you?"

"S'pose there's no harm 'oo knowing now 'oo might die an' all." That was reassuring. "Fing is, I killed one of my own kind so I'm an outcast. Don't look at me like that. He was a prick. He was goin' around killing people – humans and supernaturals. Sed they tasted better than pigeons, which shows how gone in the head he woz.

"I tried to contact the Magical Liaison Office but no one was doin' anyfink about it so one day he was sittin' up on the cathedral with me and talkin' about some tourists below he was eyein' up and I jus' cudn't take it anymore and I kills him." Gary sighed and carried on, "Problem is that killin' our own kind is sorta taboo for us gargoyles so I was about to be killed meself when Mim turns up and speaks to the elders for me. She offers up a curse instead of bein' killed as punishment and there's a chance to redeem meself if I sacrifice myself selflessly for another.

"And I finks it's a bit of a bummer, but it's better than bein' dead. So here I am. Tiny. At the mercy of anyfink bigger than a bloody pigeon and some of them are bloody aggressive an' all. So I lives with Mim and it's not so bad I s'pose. Well, till today when we might all die."

I blinked at him, trying to process his sad tale. I felt sorry for him and was about to say something when he opened his mouth and ruined it, “So whaddya fink? Fancy a snog as it might be our last day on earth an’ all?”

“Dzrak off Gary.”

I don’t know if he heard me because it was at that moment that the door blew in.

Chapter 22

The door blasted apart in a blaze of light. Jagged shards of wood flew across the room. The dark elf looked at us with a haughty gaze on his pale, grey face. Through my enchanted sunglasses, I could see the twisted rust-red of his aura.

"It's over. Go home," I tried

"Home?" he spat the word, "Home?! This was my home once. Until they turned their backs on me and forced me out to a forsaken realm to eke out a living. But I welcomed all. Every being who is shunned everywhere else. Everyone who has no home. Only what we take for ourselves." He took a step forward, drawing his sword. The serrated blade was already stained with reddish brown blood from earlier kills. His other arm hung at his side. An arrow protruded from it. It didn't seem to be slowing him down. "And I will take Avalon."

Bane seemed to grow keener in my hands. I felt the overwhelming urge to confront him in battle. My rational brain knew that was a stupid idea. That fighting him, a seasoned warrior, would only end one way. But my grip on the axe tightened. I made my choice. I wasn't going to give up on Avalon and all hope in the world without a fight.

The dark elf let loose a blast of energy that cascaded through the library. I flew backwards with force. Errol dropped from his perch on my shoulders. He whined angrily as he connected with the ground. I felt the amethyst around my neck heat, flooding me with protective energy so my spine was bruised rather than broken when I hit the bookcase. I heard the ancient tomes fall from their shelves behind me. The dark elf walked forward, dodging the magical blasts that came from the books as they hit the floor. Focused on me, he didn't see the blur of movement that sped across the room. A small rock hit the elf from the side, smashing into his stomach before bouncing to the ground. It took me a second to realise it was Gary.

"Eff off!" the gargoyle shouted before pushing himself upwards and aiming at the dark elf again. His small wings were working overtime to lift him into the air.

This time, our enemy was prepared. Magic sparked at his fingertips, and he sent a wave of it towards Gary. The small gargoyle spun in mid-air as he was sent backwards. He crashed through two bookshelves and hit the hard stone wall. I saw his small body lie still. The dark elf looked back at me, satisfied that the gargoyle threat was neutralised.

"Sheld," I muttered, using the Dwarfish word to activate the shield embedded in Bane. It gave me time to think as the dark elf pressed forward. He snarled as his magic bolts rebounded off my invisible barrier. I couldn't help but smirk as one of them reflected straight back at the magic user, forcing him to duck to one side. That's right you smug dzrakbar, hit yourself with your own evil magic.

I ran forward to try to press the advantage, but the dark elf spun round. I felt the shield falter and disappear. I had already used the magic once today and it hadn't had time to recharge. I lifted Bane to meet his serrated sword.

He was faster than me. And better trained. I reacted on instinct, blocking his attacks. He spun again and leapt behind me. I turned, less nimble, just in time to block the sword aimed at my head. It connected with the handle and my sunglasses flew from my face. I heard them crack as they hit the floor. The force of the blow rattled my arms, but thanks to the quality of the enchantments, the axe didn't break. With a snarl, the dark elf stepped forwards, pushing me back. I sent up a silent prayer to whoever might be listening. With all my strength, I twisted the axe, forcing the sword away from my face.

I aimed a kick at the dark elf's knee. My boot smacked into his kneecap with all the force I could manage. He cursed and moved away. At that small triumph, Bane sang in my hands, urging me onwards. I felt strong and powerful. Outside, the battle continued to rage but I was focused. I felt a perfect harmony and peace I hadn't known existed in violence. It was me and the axe. Together. As one.

Then the dark elf's blade came down and nicked my leg. Pain shot through me. I cried out without thinking. The creature spun and came at me again. This time his sword connected hard with my armour. I staggered under the blow.

My ribs were bruised, maybe broken. It was hard to get my breath. The axe took over.

I don't know how it happened exactly but suddenly I was standing. My arms and legs moved with a speed I definitely didn't possess by myself. I felt ancient power flow through me. I blocked the next attack, turning my axe deftly to retaliate. The dark elf stepped back from the unexpected onslaught. Bane glowed a pale blue. The runes etched into the blade and the haft blazed almost white. One seemed to be lit up stronger than the rest. Without thinking, I said the Dwarfish word for fire. The axe exploded into flames brighter than I had ever seen before. The dark elf squinted at the fiery blade and then looked at me.

"Impossible…"

My rational brain wanted to ask questions. He seemed to know something about the axe. But then Bane was back in control. I surged forward at the enemy, using moves I didn't know and hadn't ever made before. The axe seemed bloodthirsty. I closed my eyes as it aimed for his neck. I felt a dull thunk as the blade connected with something. I took a deep breath and forced my eyes open.

The axe was sunk into a bookshelf. I swore and pulled it out. Just in time to spin and block my opponent's own attack to my neck. He forced me backwards to the crystal wall. The very thing I was supposed to be protecting. My arms were starting to tire. I didn't know how much blood I had lost. Bane seemed to feel angry with me for losing power. I knew I couldn't keep up with the axe for much longer.

The dark elf sensed something was up. He renewed his attacks. Bane swung for his legs and managed to connect, sinking into his flesh. He cried out but limped forwards, forcing me to keep blocking his evil-looking sword. Then my back was to the wall. The crystals seemed to sing as I touched them. I felt the amethyst around my neck warm again. I used the power they were passing to me to feed Bane as it worked to block the attacks. But I couldn't keep up with the elf. With a cruel twist of the sword, the elf hooked his blade under one of the axe heads and yanked it from my hands. I cried out. It was a physical loss. I realised how much energy Bane had been lending me as I leant against the wall, suddenly weak.

The dark elf smiled nastily, "And so it ends."

Everything happened in slow motion. My senses stretched, trying to take in everything for the last time. The wall felt warm against my back. I sank down it, crouching on the floor, my head bent over.

A roar sounded outside, cresting over the sounds of battle. The coloured light flowing into the room through the stained glass window leant an ethereal feel to the chaos in the library. The smell of old paper and leather surrounded me. A slow trickle of blood worked its way down my arm and dripped onto the floor. I closed my eyes as the dark elf lifted his blade.

Chapter 23

As he lowered his sword, I surged upwards, stepping inside his reach. I plunged my small dagger into the soft flesh under his armpit, thanking Espretha for making me wear an ankle holster and drilling me in the importance of a backup weapon.

Mordred staggered backwards. I collapsed against the wall, watching him clutch at his shoulder. And then the room exploded. The dragon's blue head shattered the large stained glass window sending colourful panes splintering across the room. I lifted my hands protectively over my head as the shards rained down. The creature let out a roar as it entered the room. It landed hard, crushing the remains of the bookshelves. I had a crazy thought that I hoped the books were alright. The dark elf turned to stare at the beast. He lifted his sword weakly.

Unbelievably, Aloora was seated where the dark elf had been only a short time before. She spoke in draconic, the words sounding harsh and strange on her tongue. The dragon bent its neck over the dark elf and opened its mouth. He seemed small and powerless against the awesome might of the dragon. I was expecting lightning to come crackling from its throat. Instead, I heard a small scream and then the dark elf was gone.

The crunching noises that echoed from its large jaws as it devoured the dark elf will haunt my nightmares forever. My friend had a determined look in her eyes and a set to her jaw that made me want to take a step back.

The dragon turned its attention to me. Its breath stank of blood and raw meat. I blinked and held my breath as its yellow eyes examined me. Aloora spoke something in Draconic and it lowered itself so she could dismount. She ran over to me lithely and enveloped me in a hug.

"Are you alright?"

"I'm fine," the words came to me automatically. My brain caught up with the fact that the dark elf was gone. I edged around the dragon to where Gary lay prone on the floor. His small stony form was wreathed in smoke. I heard a gasp and saw a shadow growing. Then a larger version of Gary was grinning at us from the floor. "Wotcha?" he said weakly. His sacrifice had released the curse.

"Thanks Gary," I sniffed and gave him a hug. It was like hugging a boulder, unyielding and hard.

"No trouble innit," he grinned. He gave a cough. It sounded like a truck driving over gravel. Then he lay still, unmoving. Fat, wet tears dripped down my face and landed on his rocky body.

Aloora moved to stand next to me. She placed her hand on my shoulder and let me weep for the brave creature.

"Hey, I'm not dead y'know. Stop cryin' on me or I'll get moss!"

"Gary!" I sniffed, wiping snot on my sleeve. The gargoyle grumbled but he let me hug him more tightly. Then he ruined the moment.

"I didn't fink 'oo liked me like that, but if 'oo wanna dump the elf, I'm into it!"

I hit the gargoyle playfully on his arm, earning myself a sore hand. He adjusted himself so he was sitting up, grinning grotesquely.

I turned from him back to Aloora, "How are we…?" I didn't know how to finish that sentence.

"The tide has turned, and now that dzrakbar dark elf is dead, we can free the creatures. Without them, the dark elves will fall."

The dragon made a horrible noise, somewhere between a retch and a roar. It sounded like it was dying. Aloora turned with concern, "Fulgor, are you alright?"

The dragon's eyes bulged, its mouth was open as it continued its strange hacking sound. Its front feet pawed at the carpet, tearing it up as its claws sank into the thick pile. A blast of lightning shot towards us. I ducked and closed my eyes against the light. The white flash was still visible even with my eyes tight shut. A clattering sound reverberated around the room. Once the colour behind my eyes returned to a dull red, I opened them. The dragon was licking its lips and looking proud of itself.

I followed its gaze to see the serrated sword the dark elf had wielded pooled in a puddle of green drool. The lighting had left a black mark on the library's wall and a pile of books was on fire. One of the tomes seemed to be trying to fly away.

Aloora ran over to it and stamped out the fire while apologising to the semi-sentient book. It ruffled its pages and put itself away on the least crushed bookshelf with what might have been a huff. My friend picked up the sword and turned back to me, "Well if you're alright here…"

I nodded, "Don't even worry about it."

She whistled to the large dragon, who again bent its large body down so she could scramble into the harness. She managed it, even while holding the unwieldy sword. With a nod to me, she spoke in Draconic and the dragon launched itself back through the hole where the stained glass window had been, keeping its wings tight to its body.

I allowed myself to sink down against the wall and closed my eyes for a second. More than anything I wanted to fall asleep here and rest. I felt a comfortingly familiar head lay itself on my lap. I opened my eyes and scratched Errol's head. One of his wings was bent, but he was alive.

My thoughts turned to my friends, and I forced myself to stand. I walked, or more accurately, limped out of the library to somewhere where I could see the battle. I paused on one of the ramparts and stared over the horde gathered to destroy Avalon.

Aloora flew high above them on the newly freed dragon, waving the serrated sword and speaking into a radio she had found somewhere. As she swooped back and forth, showing proof of our victory, the army seemed to lose heart. A troop of trolls simply turned their backs and walked away, disappearing into the forests. I heard Mim's voice reverberate around the castle, amplified by magic.

"It is over. Your leader is dead and your dragon is free. Now all of you must make your choice. If you fight, you will lose against the forces of light and hope. If you surrender, your lives will be spared. The choice is yours. There will be a truce for one hour for you to decide."

As the last echoes of her voice disappeared, a shield appeared between the two armies. At the time, I couldn't process the horror of the battlefield. The corpses lining the ground and the fetid smell of death were a blurry fog.

Instead, my brain picked out the little things. I saw Morthimas' banner flying proud near the front line. A band of dark elves who had pushed ahead and were deep inside the army of light were suddenly cut off from their army. They realised this at the same moment and huddled together.

To our army's credit, the dwarves around them didn't mow them down and instead honoured the truce by lifting their shields and merely encircling the hapless dark elves. They kept them surrounded but unharmed.

The dark elves themselves seemed to have lost heart and some of them sat down on the trampled meadow grass while they waited for orders. The elven gryphons that had survived the fall had landed, creating a swatch of gold among the greys and blacks of the battlefield. I turned away as one of them plunged its head into the carcass of a fallen night hound. The details were hazy after that but they would come back to me in graphic detail much later.

I remember the blue dragon glinting like a sapphire in the sun as it continued to fly over the bloody chaos below. Then I blacked out.

Chapter 24

I woke up in some sort of tent. The pastel yellow fabric roof billowed in a light wind. It was strangely calming. My mouth felt like someone had poured glue into it, maybe after mixing said glue with sawdust. I was sore all over. I lay still for a little while and closed my eyes again. Maybe I could go back to sleep and wake up when there was less pain. My body and brain refused to cooperate, so I blinked my eyes open. There was more fabric hung around my bed to create some privacy. I got the impression there were more people the other side of the hangings.

Snippets from the battle ran through my brain like I was watching an action movie…Lorandir falling with the gryphon guard…Dot burned and lying unmoving on the ground…Mordred staring at me as he bled from the wound I had caused.

My chest heaved with the emotion I had been holding in. I moved to wipe away the tears and felt a hand in mine. I focused on the long slender fingers before tracking the arm with my eyes and arriving at the face of Lorandir. I tried to speak but my mouth was so dry, it came out like a croak.

"You're awake!" he bent down and enveloped me in a tight hug. I let out a cry of pain and shock. I was sure he'd been killed. He tried to release me with a sheepish look on his attractive face. I clung onto him tightly as he whispered, "Sorry."

I swallowed painfully and met his gaze, "Don't be, I thought you'd died." I hugged him again, refusing to let go as I savoured the feel of his arms around me. He pulled away, murmuring that he was getting me some water. Reluctantly, I broke apart from him and was immediately accosted by Errol trying to lick my face with his forked tongue. I tickled his ear before stroking him soothingly. His wing was bandaged but other than that he was unharmed as he did a little jump, letting me know he was excited I was still alive.

The water was cool and fresh to my parched throat. I drank it too quickly and ended up spluttering some out. The liquid dribbled down my chin and onto Errol's head. Really classy. Lorandir dabbed the water away with a square of cloth he'd got from somewhere. The look in his eyes made me want to choke again. I don't think anyone had ever regarded me with so much warmth and care. It made me forget that I must look like a complete mess. Self-consciously, I tried to smooth my wayward hair down.

"Tell me what happened," I begged, wanting to know but also afraid to hear who might be dead.

"Only if you lie back down and get some rest."

"Whatever you prescribe, doctor."

He quirked an eyebrow at me, "You must be feeling better. Barely conscious to sarcasm in less than a minute."

I shrugged and motioned for more water. He obliged and supported me while I drank before plumping up the pillow on the bed and telling me to lie down again. I sank onto the hard bed, moving Errol next to me, and Lorandir covered me with a hand-knitted woollen blanket that I recognised from the Magical Liaison Office van. Then he held my hand and I felt the reassuring golden flow of his magic surround me, healing me. I inhaled as I relaxed into the familiar sensation of honey mead and ancient forests coupled with bittersweet dark chocolate. I knew I wasn't completely healed, but I instantly felt better.

He began talking in his soft lilting accent, telling me what he thought I wanted to know. I closed my eyes and listened. I was in one of a number of hospital tents Mim had conjured after the battle. Dot was here somewhere too. My eyes shot open. I couldn't believe it. I asked him to repeat himself just so I could be sure.

She had been badly burned in her fight with the ifrit and the sunlight had stopped her being able to heal herself. But she was alive and well enough to demand her knitting needles.

Maxi and Fi had opened the portal so those residents of Avalon who couldn't fight were able to flee. They had managed to reach out to the Magical Liaison Office and reinforcements had come through armed with their standard issue crossbows and other magical weapons.

He left out the details of the battle but I could picture the horror when I closed my eyes. It was something I knew I was going to see in my dreams for a long time. The tide had already started to turn before they entered the fray and they had really ended up herding the remains of the army into containment pens while Madam Mim decided what to do with them. I closed my eyes as I listened and was soon asleep again.

When I woke again, the tent was bathed in the orangey-pink glow of sunset or sunrise. I looked to my left and saw Lorandir dozing beside me in an uncomfortable-looking wooden chair that was far too small for his tall frame. Errol was curled asleep in his lap. I smiled before remembering where I was and what had happened. I tried to think through the list of things he had told me before I passed out. He'd left out one important thing. Aloora. Was it because the worst had happened?

I dug through my pockets slowly, partly so I didn't wake the elf ,and partly because all of me still felt bruised despite Lorandir's healing magic. I found my phone eventually and tried Aloora's number. Nothing. I checked the screen. No signal. Dzraking magical interference. I wondered if Fi, the tech witch, could help me but I had no idea where she was. I shuffled on my bed, trying to sit up. My bladder reminded me it was alive and well. And full. I winced as I forced myself up and off the bed. Lorandir stirred but stayed asleep. He must be exhausted if he could sleep through my heavy tread.

I poked my head out of a gap in the hangings. There were many more pieces of fabric strung up around the tent, which was more the size of a marquee now I could see it clearly. Healers were dashing between the hastily erected partitions, and I caught the sensation of healing magic from all around. I shuffled out. One of the healers saw me and darted over.

"What are you doing up? How are you feeling?"

Another healer joined him, "You're needed over there. Spear wound to the gut. It's turning nasty." I must have paled because the new healer looked at me, "You don't look so good…hey aren't you the one who killed Mordred?"

Suddenly I was surrounded by people anxious to hear the story, "Er, actually, I didn't kill Mordred and I, er, really need the loo."

The crowd dispersed, disappointed. Someone shoved a chamber pot at me. It was porcelain and pretty to look at if you like vine decorations. But there was no way I was going to pee in that. I handed it back and started off towards what looked like an opening in the marquee walls.

One helpful healer caught up to me, gave me a dose of *Madam Mim's Cure All* and pointed me to one end of the tent. After I'd used the facilities and downed the Cure All, I felt a lot better, even with the sticky aniseed aftertaste in my mouth. I started to make my way back to my 'room' when a familiar voice caught my ear.

"So, you just yarn over a final time then pull the thread through all the loops and voila!"

"I see, and what did you call that stitch again?"

"Ball stitch, and you may have to give it a teeny push to make sure all the balls are on the same side, but that's easy enough."

I poked my head through the hanging curtain, "What are you ballsing up in here?"

Dot gave me a toothy grin, showing off her fangs. I fought back tears of relief. She looked like she had a bad case of sunburn and was wrapped in several blankets but otherwise seemed entirely fine. The way she was speeding through her current crochet project, she might even have made all those blankets while she was in the hospital tent.

On a chair next to her sat one of the Omensford witches, crochet hook in hand and a ball of bright yellow wool sitting on her lap. Her white hair was pulled into an elegant French twist and looked orange in the light from the lamp on the table. She was wearing a neat cardigan and skirt combination with a string of pearls sitting around her neck. Both women held up their crochet projects. It looked like Dot was working on yet another blanket, with little bobbles that I guessed were meant to be the ball stitches. The witch had a yellow square on hers, with an intricate diamond lacy pattern but no balls as yet.

"And how are you?" the vampire asked as she continued to dip and weave her crochet hook into the blue wool, "I heard you fought Mordred and won."

"Er, well I did fight Mordred but it wasn't exactly like I won..." I turned my thoughts away from that fight. I still wasn't sure exactly what had happened except my friend had shown up on a dzraking dragon. "Have you seen Aloora?"

"I think she was with Maxi. He was getting looked over for electric burns last I heard."

The witch tsked, "My daughter should learn to control her power, she gets over excited."

I studied the older witch's face as she continued. There were some similarities in the shape of the eyes and the cheekbones between her and the tech witch. She paused and looked at me expectantly. I blinked.

"Sorry, I didn't catch that…"

"I was saying thank you for saving my daughter's life. Fiona was quite clear that without you turning up she and this Maxi would likely be dead. You'll have to come and stay with us in Omensford as a thank you. I run a small bed and breakfast there, you're welcome to come any time."

"Er, thank you, that's really kind."

"Not at all, consider it a small gesture of gratitude. Here, take my card," the witch handed me a small rectangle of card that read: *Omensford Bed & Breakfast, rooms for your every desire* with a phone number printed below.

"Thank you…"

"Eleanor, Eleanor Blair, but please call me Nell and do call me to arrange your stay."

"Thank you Ele…Nell. I'm going to find Aloora now. Are you alright Dot, do you need anything?"

The vampire shook her head, gestured to the IV full of blood that was connected to her arm and bent back over her crochet blanket. I backed out of the cubicle and kept walking.

"Yah, that's a row for me!" Maxi's unmistakably loud and excited voice sounded across the marquee. I followed the elongated vowels to his cubicle and coughed loudly before announcing myself. "Yah, yah come in!"

Maxi was sat up on his bed, looking a little dishevelled. His hair normally stuck out a bit but since his electric shock, it was on end, exactly like a mad professor. He waved at me and then turned back to the game board set out on a stool between him and Agent Jones. They were taking turns to place white or black disks next to others, which turned the neighbouring counters the same colour. Othello I think it's called. Agent Jones looked up at me.

"You're alright then."

It wasn't a question, but I answered anyway, "Yeah, I'm fine. Bruised but fine."

"Well done on fighting Mordred, he was a powerful sorcerer."

I thought back to our fight, "Yeah, I got that. He's gone now though. What happened to his army?"

"They're being allowed to return to their homes peacefully for the most part. Mim and Arthur are handling the details and the Office is working on warrants for any of them who decide to come to earth unannounced."

"That's a lot of warrants!"

"Yep. Good job Maxi needs the company, or I'd have to be involved in that paperwork."

Maxi gave me a wink as he set down another piece in a corner of the board and claimed a row. Agent Jones let out a growl of frustration.

I clamped my lips together to keep in the laugh that was threatening to escape from my mouth.

"What do you want anyway?" Agent Jones' eyes were back on the game.

"I thought Aloora was in here."

“She’s outside with Mim,” Agent Jones turned her counter over and over in her fingers, eyeing the board. She placed it carefully and flipped a couple of Maxi’s pieces over with a triumphant smile. Maxi placed his own disk and instantly returned the newly turned pieces back to his colour. I left as Agent Jones swore.

“It’s a stupid kids’ game anyway!”

I waited until I was outside to let out the giggle that had been bubbling in my throat at Agent Jones losing to Maxi at a simple board game. I’d have to try to set up a games night for us all when we were back in Cardiff.

Once outside the roomy tent, Aloora was easy to spot. Because she was the only one brave, or stupid, enough to be close to a dragon. The creature was lying down next to the castle. Its blue scales were enchantingly iridescent in the sunset. An image of a jewelled necklace came into my mind: gold with inset sapphires or possibly mother of pearl to capture the ethereal quality of the dragon in the light. I pulled out my phone. There was still no signal, but the camera worked, and I snapped a picture.

The quality wasn’t as good on the screen, but it would help jog my memory when I wanted to create that piece. My fingers itched at the thought of being back in my workshop. Strangely, it wasn’t my old shop that was still being repaired from the arson attack or my rented bench in Gunther’s warehouse that filled my head.

It was my old shed back at Mum and Dad’s place, where I had first started creating jewellery under the watchful and patient gaze of my father, the master craftsdwarf. I imagined what my parents would be doing of a winter evening.

A pang of homesickness hit me. Mum would be watching one of her programmes, probably a crime drama or possibly another home design programme that drove my Dad mad. Dad would be drinking and pretending not to watch it or else pottering about in his own workshop until Mum shouted to him that he was disturbing the neighbours. We all knew that he'd put a silencing spell over his workshop, but it was the traditional way to get him back in the house or else he'd be likely to fall asleep with his tools. I shook my head. Get back to the present Ame. Cautiously, I approached my friend and the dragon.

She saw me first and ran over. The tight squeeze had me wincing, but I was feeling a lot better.

"Did you really ride a dragon or was I hallucinating?"

Aloora's eyes gleamed as she looked over at the massive reptile, "I really rode him. Isn't he gorgeous? His name's …" my friend let out a series of coughs and growls that made me pat her on the back. "Get off! I'm not choking, that's his name!"

"Er, OK," mentally I named the dragon Blue.

"And how were you riding him?"

"Well, there was this cruel saddle thing attached to him and I took it off…"

"You went up to it!"

"I couldn't let him suffer! Anyway, I've been practising my Draconic and so I spoke to him and managed to get off all the awful spikes and the collar was much too tight. I asked him to help us get revenge on the one who had done this to him, and he allowed me to ride him. It was incredible!"

"Er…"

"You have to try it Ame! It's the most amazing feeling!"

"Er…maybe some other time."

"Of course, of course. And how are you?"

"Don't even worry about it, I've had healing potions and everything. I'm fine."

"Good, come on, I want you to meet him," the petite gnome dragged me over to her new dragon-friend and spoke something in Draconic. The dragon opened his mouth. I flinched but instead of a flash of lightning, he appeared to be responding to Aloora. She said something back and then translated for me. "He says hello."

"That's it?" It seemed like a long-winded way of saying hello.

"He also said he's happy for you to ride him with me."

"Er, thanks I guess," the dragon's eyes glinted in the sunlight as Aloora translated my thanks, "But not right now!" I added as his head snaked towards us. Aloora patted his scales and, reluctantly, I did the same. He felt warm to touch and smooth under my hand. Not unlike Errol. He made a crooning noise then opened his wings and took off. The downdraught made me duck from the force.

"He's gone hunting," Aloora smiled.

"I never thought I'd see you infatuated with a man!" That earned me a punch to my upper arm. "Ouch, sorry."

"He's not a man, he's a dragon! Now come on, Mim wants to see you."

Chapter 25

Aloora led me into the great hall. The long tables and benches were still there but there was a large pig roasting in the open fireplace and the atmosphere felt a lot more upbeat than when we had been supping on oats before the battle. I caught sight of a group of dwarves having what I was fairly certain was a drinking competition at one end of a table. I turned back to catch up with my friend when one of the dwarves got up and strode over to me. I recognised the neatly trimmed beard and precise step of Ironfist. He was still in his armour, although his war hammer was resting against one of the walls near his drinking buddies.

“Amethyst, I’m glad I caught you,” we shook hands with the traditional forearm grasp greeting that dwarves use, “I hear it’s thanks to you that we are rid of that cocht-wimble Mordred and his evil sorcery.”

“Er, I don’t know who’s been saying that but…”

He cut me off, “Now I’ll be putting in a word with the Dwarven Arms Council so you can expect to hear from us soon.”

I smiled blankly as Ironfist clasped my forearm again before starting to head back to his drink. The last thing I wanted was to come to the attention of the Dwarven Arms Council. Again.

Earlier this year they had selected me to be their delegate at the Equinox Ball and, in return for them paying for a bespoke designer ball gown, I'd had to suffer through small talk and nearly got killed by a dragon. Although I supposed the dragon wasn't really their fault.

"And another thing," the small dwarf turned back mid pace, "I've been meaning to talk to you about that axe of yours."

I instinctively reached for the handle. My ancestral axe had been one of the reasons the Dwarven Arms Council had been interested in me in the first place. Apparently, it was taboo for dwarf-made weapons to be passed down to half-breeds. Dad had promised me he'd sent in the paperwork transferring ownership…My throat dried up.

"I have found some very interesting lineage…"

"Come on Ame, Mim is waiting. I'm sorry to butt in Ironfist…"

"Not at all, not at all. Perhaps now is not the time in any case," the dwarf executed a clipped bow, "Good day to you both and I will be seeing you Ms Haernson."

Aloora dragged me out of the hall while I asked myself why his words seemed more like a threat than a goodbye. She hustled me into the cosy study we had been led to when we had first arrived in Avalon. So much had happened since then. So much that I wanted to forget seeing.

Madam Mim set aside an ancient map she was studying and rose from her comfy red chair to greet us. King Arthur was standing to one side. He had removed his armour and was instead sporting cream-coloured breeches and a long woollen smock, also in cream but with gold thread embroidered through it. I squinted at the design over his chest. A dragon. Arthur Pendragon, of course. Slung on his sword belt, I saw Excalibur's jewelled scabbard glinting in the light from the candles.

"Welcome, both of you," Mim started, "I offer you Avalon's thanks for saving us from Mordred's scheme. Had he succeeded, well, it doesn't bear speaking of."

"Don't even worry about it," the words came out automatically. I blushed under Mim's arched eyebrow as soon as they came out of my mouth.

"Indeed. Well then let me extend my personal gratitude for saving my home and many lives with your timely actions. I want to grant you citizenship of Avalon. You are welcome here any time you wish to visit the realm."

A warm trickling sensation washed through me as Mim said the words. I'd been magically granted citizenship into a fae realm.

"Er, well it was more Aloora and that dzraking, I mean, really huge dragon," Aloora nudged me in the ribs to stop me talking.

"Yes, congratulations Ms Dragonquest for being the first natural dragon rider in several millennia. I understand you have been able to communicate with the lightning dragon?"

I wanted to ask why they weren't considering Mordred the first dragon rider in millennia, but it didn't seem like the right time. Aloora nodded enthusiastically, "Yes, it's fascinating really, the form of Draconic is similar to that of the other dragons awakened recently but not exactly the same. I'm trying to find out where he comes from and…" It was my turn to nudge my friend in the ribs. She assumed everyone was as big a dragon nerd as her.

"We must discuss what you are going to do with your dragon…" Madam Mim nodded her head at Arthur and he walked towards me and offered me his arm. I looked between Mim and Aloora but they had already bent their heads over the map that covered the table top.

I accepted Arthur's arm and allowed him to escort me out of the room.

"I have questions," I blurted as he matched his longer steps to mine.

He looked down at me, an amused look on his face, "I imagine thee doth." My brows crinkled in confusion at his antiquated speech. "Well, speak thy questions."

"What will happen to all those creatures in Mordred's army? Agent Jones said they were leaving peacefully…"

"Aye, they will leave in peace after we hath finished questioning them. We hath no quarrel with them and many were ensorcelled," he saw my confusion again and sighed before explaining, "under Mordred's spell. Those who were unaware of their actions may go. Those who chose to join him need further consideration."

I nodded thoughtfully, then asked my second question, "Why does she go by Madam Mim and not Morgan le Fay?"

He laughed, his bushy eyebrows lifting in merriment, "'Tis not for me to answer that riddle. Ask her thyself."

I paused. There was one more thing I wanted to ask, but it seemed too presumptuous. I was on the brink of asking several times as Arthur led me back through the courtyard and towards the hospital tent. I finally summoned up my courage and opened my mouth to speak. I was interrupted by a relieved shout.

"Amethyst! There you are! You were gone when I awoke!"

I turned to see Lorandir running towards us, worry filling his green eyes. Errol was curled around his neck and the wind tousled the elf's short blonde hair, so it looked like he was in some sort of bad music video from the nineties.

"Er, sorry, I just went to find Aloora."

"You could have said something!" he swept me into a hug. I grimaced slightly. The *Cure All* hadn't managed to dispel all the bruising.

"You looked so peaceful when you were sleeping."

"I will leave thee two and bid thee good day," Arthur turned and began striding away with long paces.

I shifted from side to side in Lorandir's arms before making my decision, "Hey, Arthur…I mean King Arthur, your majesty?"

The tall warrior turned and raised one bushy eyebrow in my direction.

"Could I, er, if it's not too much trouble, er, can I see Excalibur?" I rushed the end of the sentence.

The King smiled and unstrung the sword in its scabbard from his waist. He turned it and lay it across his hands as he offered it to me. I moved forward. I was keen to see the sword, but it demanded some sort of reverence.

I moved my hands over the scabbard, feeling the magic wrought into it. It was leather, coated with a thin layer of gold, into which precious jewels had been set. I recognised the familiar deep purple amethysts that matched the one hanging around my neck. There were others too; rich red rubies, clear diamonds, deep green emeralds and pale sapphires, all lending their innate power to the wearer.

Near the top, I could sense enchantments that had been woven into certain jewels for healing and protection. I wished I had my enchanting goggles with me so I could see the intricate magic. It was old and sophisticated and, according to legend, meant that the wearer of the scabbard could not be killed. I noticed a space near the point of the scabbard where a jewel had come loose.

"I could replace that for you," I murmured before realising I had been presumptuous enough to offer to fix a legendary artefact, "I mean…er…"

Arthur gave a short bark of laughter, "The scabbard doth fulfil its purpose without all the decoration. That jewel was cut off centuries ago and I hope I will not see many more battles. Thank thee for thy kindness and if ever it has need of repair, I pray thee will honour thine offer. But, me thinks 'twas the blade thee wanted to see."

I nodded and reached for the handle. There was one large red ruby on the pommel and the handle was wrapped with brown leather binding for better grip. It felt large in my small hand. The power of it snaked through my grip and up my arm with a warm sensation like hot dripping honey; thick, viscous and sweet. I looked up at Arthur for confirmation I could really draw the legendary blade. He nodded at me kindly and twisted his grip, so it was easier for me to pull the sword from its scabbard.

The sword sung as I drew it free. I sighted along the blade. It was well made, fashioned from blue steel that gleamed like the surface of a puddle of oil as I turned it in the twilight of Avalon's multi-coloured sky. I moved the sword gently in a couple of mock swipes.

As I expected, it was perfectly balanced. It felt light in my hand, an extension of my body. I suspected that was part of the sword's magic. I felt strong and powerful. I knew the sword would guide me in battle, repelling blows before I even saw them coming and smiting my enemies. It was intoxicating. I longed for a fight so I could try it out. I found myself wondering why Arthur didn't wield it all the time. I had felt something akin to that in the battle with Mordred when Bane had seemed to fight for me.

As I thought of my ancestral axe, my free hand reached subconsciously for its blade. Somewhere, deep inside my mind, a small voice whispered maybe this was why Arthur kept it sheathed until it was needed. I met the King's cold blue eyes.

There was a look of understanding in them. I marvelled at the willpower he needed to carry such a powerful weapon at his side without it taking him over. Suddenly, it felt more dangerous than awe-inspiring. The rational part of my brain was back in control, and I carried on my inspection. Carefully, I touched my finger to the blade. It was sharp. I sucked on my bloody finger and swore without thinking before apologising to the King.

" 'Tis not something to apologise for. I should have warned thee; Excalibur seeks blood. It keeps the blade sharp. But, 'twill only take life in righteous battle."

I felt a hand on my shoulder and then the warm sensation of Lorandir's healing magic swept through me and focused on my finger in the familiar feeling of leafy forests, honey mead and bittersweet dark chocolate. It was a bit over the top for a tiny cut, but I appreciated it nonetheless, and my bruised body went from deep pain to a dull ache as his magic flowed through the rest of me.

The sword almost hummed in my hand. I closed my eyes and tried to pick out the different spells cast on it. I recognised some but there were others foreign to me.

"I thought this was dwarf-forged?"

King Arthur nodded, " 'Twas, so I am told."

"But I can sense fae magic too," the sticky sensation of fae curled along the blade, sharpening and amplifying the dwarven enchantments.

"I doth not know all the secrets of the sword. 'Twas gifted to me by a lady of the lake a long time ago…" his eyes misted over with a fond memory and a smile curled his lips up before he continued, "…and re-gifted to me when I retired from the human world and came to rest here in Avalon." He held out the scabbard for the sword and I returned it to its rightful place. It slipped inside the jewelled scabbard effortlessly and the magic ebbed out of me.

I bowed my head to King Arthur, "Thank you for allowing me that honour."

"'Twas but a small request for the saviour of Avalon," with a nod, King Arthur turned and strode back into the castle.

"But I didn't save Avalon," I protested but he didn't acknowledge me. I leant against Lorandir, getting comfort from his lean body. He massaged my shoulders, sending his healing magic through me again. I sighed with pleasure.

"What do you want to do now, my love?"

I looked up at the swirling ethereal colours of the fae sky. It was magical, but there was nothing more to do here. I thought of my family. My Mum and Dad, Uncle Owain and Dylan. More than anything, I wanted to see them again.

I wanted to taste Mum's awful attempts at dwarven food and Dylan's excellent pastries. I wanted to argue with them over family board games. For the first time in a long time, I longed to be at home. Not independent in my own shop or living with my friends. I wanted to spend time with my family. I looked up into Lorandir's green eyes, "You know, I think I want to go home."

Epilogue

I stalled the car as I pulled up outside my family home. Marco had leant us his ancient Volkswagen while he was back in Italy for Christmas, and I had cursed the old car and its sticky windscreen wipers the whole journey. We couldn't even listen to any decent music as the radio was permanently tuned to BBC Radio Four and I was starving after hearing about alternative Christmas roasts for the last hour. I slammed the door shut behind me as I got out of the piece of junk car. It made a satisfying clunk followed by a thud as something came loose inside. Schiztz.

"Hey, don't take it out on the car!"

Lorandir had been keeping me sane on the journey by passing me jelly sweets that we had bought for an extortionate price at one of the garages on the way. They hadn't filled the hole in my stomach.

The elf exited the car more sedately and allowed Errol to climb onto his shoulders. The small wyrm settled himself quickly and looked around from his new vantage point. Since he'd spent time with Marco, Errol had decided he preferred to sit around the necks of tall men, and I was now his third choice after both Marco and Lorandir.

Still grumbling, I started to unload presents from the boot of the car. Lorandir grabbed the suitcases while I struggled to pile the oddly shaped gifts on top of each other, so I only needed to make one trip to the front door. I finally managed to balance everything and shut the boot when I realised Lorandir was already pushing the doorbell. Schiztz.

I hurried across the lawn, ignoring the paved path that curved decoratively across the grass, but was a longer route. I felt my foot slip on the wet grass. Schiztz. I didn't fall thanks to my heavy-duty gothic style boots and their large tread, but I dropped a couple of the presents. Swearing again, I bent to retrieve them and lost more to the ground.

"Dzrak it all!"

"Amethyst! Language please!" I looked up to see my mother had opened the door and was staring at me with disapproval on her immaculately made-up face. Schiztz. I mumbled my apologies and hurried over, but it was too late. She had already enveloped Lorandir in a hug and then stood back to admire the elf.

"It's so lovely to finally meet you in person Lorandir, am I saying it right? I don't know why Amethyst has kept us away for so long," she aimed another disapproving glare at me, "you're so handsome. Come in, come in." Mum ushered the elf inside, still talking.

I stood on the threshold, still struggling with my depleted pile of presents. I dumped them just inside the door and went to rescue the brightly coloured packages that littered the lawn.

"Shut the door behind you, would you love?" Mum called from somewhere in the house.

"Don't worry about welcoming me, your only daughter or offering to help, oh no," I mumbled as I

closed the wooden door more forcefully than I would normally.

"Now, now love, she's just excited to meet your boyfriend," I turned and met Dad's eyes, brown like my own and sparkling with humour. I rushed to give him a hug.

"Merry Christmas Dad!"

"And to you, now let me look at you," he stepped back and pretended to study me, "a new haircut?"

I shook my head with a smile, "Nothing's changed Dad." I started to take off my boots and placed them next to the shoe rack just inside the door.

"Well you've definitely lost weight, we'll have to do something about that over the holidays!"

"Dad!"

"Alright, alright," he held his hands out, "Why don't I get you a drink while your mother finishes terrorising the elf?"

I shoved some of the presents into his arms before grabbing the remaining gifts and following him into the lounge. The large fir tree dominated the entire room. Mum and Dad had gone all out this year and clearly selected the biggest tree they could find.

The flickering lights made it look magical as they reflected off the silvery tinsel and mirrored baubles. I placed the presents under the tree where they somehow looked more inviting and intriguing, even though I knew exactly what was in them. My hair caught on a branch as I straightened and came nose to nose with a hideous paper Father Christmas. Now I looked more closely, I could see the tree was strung with embarrassing homemade decorations that I vaguely remembered making as a child.

"Ugh, did you have to hang those?"

"We're proud of all your achievements love, even when your clay reindeers look like an animal's done its business." Dad lifted a brown lump of salt dough hung on a red string to show me how bad that had been.

"In my defence, I was only five!"

"Don't let your Dad tease you Ame, you should see some of the rubbish he made growing up! I think I've still got the helmet that looks like it was made for a mutant bear!"

"Uncle Owain!" I flung myself at my Uncle. His eyebrows were missing again, and he bore some fresh burn marks on his cheek, but he was cheerful as ever. The wyrms never seemed to appreciate the sanctuary they had at his wyrm farm. I took in the truly hideous Christmas jumper he was sporting with a grin. A reindeer in a pink sweater was dancing next to a Christmas tree somehow knitted from real tinsel. He had outdone himself this year.

"I suppose Dafydd hasn't offered you a drink yet?" Owain shoved a vodka and coke into my hand. I thanked him and took a sip before starting to choke.

"How much booze did you put in there?"

Owain shrugged, making the reindeer on his Christmas jumper move, "Dylan is making the drinks."

I should have known. My Uncle's other half was always overdoing the alcohol. I made my way to the kitchen to dilute my drink and say hello. Dylan was stirring something on the stove, and he turned when I entered, almost blinding me with the neon yellow stars on his own hand-made Christmas jumper. He had threaded baubles into his plaited hair, and they jangled as he took the few steps across the kitchen to sweep me into a bear hug.

"Glad you could make it! Is your fancy man here?" he looked around as if I was somehow hiding a six-foot something elf behind my five foot nothing frame.

"He's with Mum."

"Ah, well never mind, I've made him a special cocktail to take the edge off when he gets downstairs."

"What's in it?" I was always nervous of Dylan's alcoholic creations.

"Not much," he reassured me before proceeding to list off a number of spirits that didn't rightly belong together.

"I think he'll be alright with just some mulled wine if you've made any?"

Dylan looked affronted, "Of course I have! It's my special recipe with an extra kick." He ladled a liquid so deep red it was almost purple into a mug and handed it to me. I sniffed cautiously. It smelled delicious, the Christmas spices filling me with warmth and nostalgia. I took a sip and was pleased that the wine tasted rich and sweet. Whatever was in the concoction was good. I poured another glass for Lorandir and snuck a mince pie before heading off to save my boyfriend from Mum's questioning.

I found them upstairs in my old bedroom. It had been redecorated in one of Mum's spates of interior design. I guessed she had been aiming for a ritzy hotel look but somewhere along the way it had turned into borderline burlesque house. Trying not to focus on the heavily patterned wallpaper, I stood in the doorway and studied Mum and Lorandir for a second. I was clearly too late. The elf was blinking at something Mum had said and looking at the window as if it was a viable exit. Time to interrupt.

"Here Lorandir," I thrust the mulled wine into his hand.

"Amethyst! No coloured drinks upstairs!"

I looked down at the maroon carpet. It's not like a red wine stain would show even if there was a spill. But I played along, "Let's get downstairs then, everyone's ready to eat." By everyone, I meant me.

Mum looked horrified, "Presents first!" She raced downstairs to usher everyone into the lounge.

I patted Lorandir's hand reassuringly and led him downstairs. The poor elf still looked a bit shell-shocked.

When we got to the lounge, Mum was patting the sofa next to her and looking meaningfully at Lorandir. I decided to spare him; I misinterpreted her gesture and sank into the seat.

"Ugh, there's not enough room for you Amethyst!"

"Nonsense, just squeeze up."

Lorandir sank gratefully onto the floor next to me as Uncle Owain and Dylan had taken up the other sofa with Errol curled up between them. Dad was sitting in his own armchair with a pint of beer in his hand. Once we were all settled, he began handing out the brightly wrapped parcels, placing them in small piles in front of each of us. I eyed a lumpy looking present suspiciously. It was wrapped in paper that had small dragons printed in rows. The dragons were wearing Santa hats.

"Ooo, that's from us! Open that first!" Dylan leaned forward in his seat excitedly.

The rest of us exchanged looks and ripped open the paper on identical squashy packages to reveal personalised knitted jumpers. I fingered the fabric. It was soft and would no doubt be too warm for me. I didn't know how Dylan and Owain were wearing theirs when the wood burner was blazing.

"Well, put them on!"

I tugged mine over my head. It featured a tree hung with bright purple baubles. Not too bad if you ignored the pink plastic jewels sewn onto it. Then I caught sight of the sequined text: Merry elf-mas. There was no way I was wearing this all day.

I looked around. Mum and Dad had matching Mr and Mrs Santa jumpers, completed with fake fur trim. My face froze. Lorandir's featured a dzraking Christmas elf outfit. With dangly legs stitched on, turned up boots and all. How offensive could my family be?

Lorandir gave a forced laugh and gamely tugged it on. His head appeared through the neck hole, so it looked like he was in one of those cut out picture opportunity things you get at the seaside, normally with a cartoonish picture of a strongman printed on them. Except in this case, it was a stereotypical Christmas elf. I thrust another package into his hands to distract him.

"Here, open this."

"First, we need a family photo!" Mum stood with her digital camera in hand. She lined us all up in front of the tree and then spent five minutes angling the camera to get us all in. After the first photo, Lorandir offered to kneel next to me so his head could be in the frame and the height disparity between him and the rest of the family wasn't so obvious. After ten timed photos, Mum pronounced herself happy. Then Dylan decided he wanted to take pictures of each of the couples with his phone. After twenty minutes we were done. I forwarded the picture Dylan took of Lorandir and I to Aloora and Marco.

Merry Christmas x

Aloora sent through a crying laughing face at our jumpers and then sent a picture of her and Professor Elrond. They were bundled up in thick coats in the Breconian forest. They had decided to use the holiday season to study dragons together and get some primary data for Aloora's PhD. I smiled. I bet both of them had forgotten it was even Christmas day. Marco replied with his own family photo. I hadn't realised he had so many brothers and sisters. They looked a lot more relaxed and weren't sporting hideous jumpers.

The rest of the presents were much less lurid than the jumpers. I opened a box of luxury assortment chocolates as soon as I unwrapped it and scoffed three before offering them round. I was pleased that Mum and Dad enjoyed the gift certificate Lorandir and I had got them for a trip to the Omensford bed and breakfast. Mum would like the fact it was owned by a witch, and I'd looked up nearby pubs so I knew Dad would enjoy lunch in the local.

Presents unwrapped, Dylan and Mum retreated to the kitchen and Lorandir and I went to set the table while Dad disappeared into the garden. I put the cutlery out and arranged the red and gold crackers in front of each setting while Lorandir folded the napkins into flowers. When I asked him where he'd learnt to do that, he shrugged. He and I had had very different upbringings.

I finished placing the tiny ceramic Christmas trees Mum had told me to use as a centrepiece and stepped back to admire our efforts. Pleased that the table looked suitably festive, I snagged a seat along one side and gestured for Lorandir to sit next to me.

Mum swept in carrying a hot serving dish, "Move those! I need space!"

I pursed my lips but decided not to spoil the Christmas spirit by saying anything as I moved the small Christmas trees Mum had insisted we needed off the table. She bustled back into the kitchen.

Dad appeared and began pouring wine into everyone's glasses. I noticed we had the cut glass goblets out, as it was a special occasion. Once all the dishes were on the table and we were all seated, Dad carved the turkey and carefully counted out the prized pigs in blankets before handing out the plates.

"Schweinstopf?" Mum offered me the traditional dwarven dish.

I hesitated. Mum tried hard to make dwarven food for Dad but didn't often succeed and on occasion it had been inedible, "Er…"

"I made it, family recipe," Dylan offered with a wink that Mum didn't see. With that reassurance, I helped myself to a generous portion.

"Lorandir, I had to look up some traditional elven recipes for the holidays. I didn't know what you'd like so I made a selection," she pointed to four smaller dishes filled with various shades of goop. Lorandir paled but smiled and elf-fully took a portion of each. I dished him up some of the more traditional fare as well so he wouldn't starve. "I have to say the fish dish was pretty tricky, but I think I managed it."

I eyed the pink stuff and decided not to try any. I had bad memories of the paste when it had been made properly by elves. Dylan however took a large mouthful and almost gagged. He covered it well with a gulp of wine and then fed the rest of his portion to Errol who had followed us in and curled up under the table waiting for scraps. Uncle Owain shot him a disapproving look; he had strong views on wyrm diets.

Conversation slowed as we all ate our food. I relaxed back as I stuffed the last bacon-covered sausage into my mouth and placed my knife and fork on my plate. Lorandir cleared his plate, but I noticed he didn't go back for seconds of the elven delicacies.

"Thank you Mrs Haernson, Dylan, I don't think I could eat another bite!" the elf smiled and patted his stomach.

"Please, call me Sally. And don't be silly, there's still pudding!"

She bustled back into the kitchen with Dylan hot on her heels. Dad and Owain cleared the dishes. I patted Lorandir's hand and thanked him for trying Mum's speciality cooking. One day she'd stick to the human dishes she knew well.

Dad sat back down, brandishing a bottle of brandy and a huge metal ladle. He grinned as Mum placed a huge Christmas pudding before him, loaded the ladle with the spirit and spoke the Dwarfish word for fire. He must have overdone the magic because instead of lighting up with blue flames, the brandy shot a fireball into the ceiling. Mum stood and flapped a tea towel at the smoke as the fire alarm started to beep. Owain went to disconnect it. I heard a horrible choking sound from underneath the table.

I peered under the tablecloth to see Errol being sick all over the cream carpet. It was a frothy pink colour. The elven food hadn't agreed with him. With a sigh, I lifted the small wyrm and carried him outside to finish puking. Mum glowered at my pet as I passed her. With precision timing, he threw up again. This time all over me. I decided it wasn't all bad. At least now I had a legitimate excuse for taking off the boiling sweater.

Before I changed, I cleaned up the puddle of sick and then sprayed the carpet with stain remover. Lorandir offered to help and managed to get some of the vile liquid on his own awful jumper. He gave me a wink as he took off the offensive elf sweater.

Once we'd cleaned up, we decided to skip the flaming brandy and just have the pudding as it was. Thick, sticky and full of boozy fruit. Delicious.

Pudding finished, we cleared the table and headed back into the lounge. Dad topped off our drinks on the way out and helped himself to another bottle of beer.

"Games!" Uncle Owain declared.

We spent a good fifteen minutes deciding what to play. We ruled out traditional dwarven games like Rummy on the basis it wasn't fair to Lorandir who didn't know the rules and Mum didn't want any more flaming drinks in the house. In the end, we decided to go with charades in couples. By the fourth round, Lorandir and I were in front thanks to his acting out *Lord of the Rings.* Mum had nearly fainted when she had thought he'd been proposing to me as he got on one knee to mime 'ring', but she'd recovered and we'd won the points.

Now, however, Lorandir's eyes were starting to glaze over from the many refills of his drink. We needed this for the win. I studied my clue hard before nodding at Uncle Owain, who turned the timer. I tried pointing to the tree.

"The Christmas Tree?"

I pointed to the tree more vigorously.

"O Christmas Tree?"

I grabbed my half eaten box of chocolates and waved it at him.

"Chocolate?"

I signed two words at him again, although it may have looked like I was swearing. Then I started running on the spot.

"Chocolate running?"

I pointed to the tree again.

"Christmas marathon?"

I tried to go for a 'sounds like' clue and was miming a hump on my back when the time ran out.

"Forrest Gump!"

"Oh. I've never seen it," he took another sip of drink. I stared at him. How can anyone not have seen Forrest Gump?!

After that Dylan and Owain won the game when Dylan guessed Dragonheart almost immediately after Uncle Owain pointed to his own heart. Must have been some sort of pet name for each other. I shook my head and packed up the cards.

"The hot tub should be warm enough now. I turned it on just before lunch. Anyone fancy a dip?"

I stared at my Dad. There was no way I was getting into a warm bath with my parents. Dylan and Owain seemed up for it though and took their drinks outside onto the newly built decking. Mum and Dad joined them. I hoped they had swimming costumes out there. The alternative didn't bear thinking about. Luckily the oversized Christmas tree blocked the hot tub from view.

Alone at last, I snuggled into Lorandir and we settled down to watch my favourite Christmas film: *Nightmare Before Christmas.*

Thank you

A massive thank you as ever to my awesome husband who is not only supportive but is also the first person to read any of my stories.

And a huge thank you to my patreon supporter: Emma Ward, who always believes in me.

To my terrific typo hunters and brilliant beta readers, you made this story better than it started.

And to you, wonderful reader, thank you for picking up this book and even reading the thank you page – you are amazing!

If you enjoyed this book, you can get a free prequel to my Rise of Dragons series by signing up to my mailing list on www.gemmaclatworthy.com. And join the conversation at Gemma's book wyrms or see all my books before they're published on patreon.com /G_Clatworthy.

As an independent author, your reviews help me decide which series to keep going so please do leave one for Attack on Avalon and if you enjoyed this book, try Fated Bloodlines, book six in the Rise of the Dragons series.

About the Author

Gemma started writing during the 2020 lockdown and loves fantasy fiction and dragons in particular. She lives in Wiltshire with her family and two cats and also enjoys crafts of all kinds. You can see all her writing on patreon.com/G_Clatworthy. Join the conversation at Gemma's book wyrms readers' group on Facebook.

She also writes children's books. You can find out more on her website www.gemmaclatworthy.com or follow her on Instagram (www.instagram.com/gemmaclatworthy) or Facebook (www.facebook.com/gemmaclatworthy).

Other Books by G Clatworthy

Books in the Rise of the Dragons series:

Awakening

Solstice of Dragons

Equinox Betrayal

Darkest Deception

Attack on Avalon

Fated Bloodlines

Books in the Omensford series (set in the Rise of Dragons universe) [Coming Autumn 2022]:

Bedsocks and Broomsticks

Cream Teas and Crystal Balls

Daughters and Demons

Children's Books

The Child Who series:

- The Girl Who Lost Her Listening Ears
- The Boy Who Lost His Listening Ears
- The Girl Who Dreamed of Sleep
- The Boy Who Dreamed of Sleep

Other books:

Coronavirus in the words of children

www.ingramcontent.com/pod-product-compliance
Ingram Content Group UK Ltd.
Pitfield, Milton Keynes, MK11 3LW, UK
UKHW040005200726
13854UKWH00001B/51

9 781915 516008